"Yo
to
with you."

"I only did all that because I knew you wouldn't
dance with me otherwise," Scott told Amanda.
"And I couldn't let that happen."

"Why not?"

"Because, Amanda, I've wanted to hold you from
the moment I saw you. Because you are, without
a doubt, the most beautiful woman I've ever laid
eyes on and I'm dying to kiss you again."

He felt her body tense, saw the way her eyes
swept back and forth between his own as if
wanting to avoid his gaze, but unable to do so.

He kissed her, not as Scott the nice guy. Not as
Scott the geek.

But as Scott the man.

And she was lost.

COWBOY LESSONS
Pamela Britton

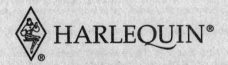

HARLEQUIN®

TORONTO • NEW YORK • LONDON
AMSTERDAM • PARIS • SYDNEY • HAMBURG
STOCKHOLM • ATHENS • TOKYO • MILAN • MADRID
PRAGUE • WARSAW • BUDAPEST • AUCKLAND

Dedicated to
Laura Blake Peterson
The best agent a writer could ever ask for.

ISBN 0-373-16985-X

COWBOY LESSONS

Copyright © 2003 by Pamela Britton.

This edition published by arrangement with Harlequin Books S.A.

® and TM are trademarks of the publisher. Trademarks indicated with
® are registered in the United States Patent and Trademark Office, the
Canadian Trade Marks Office and in other countries.

Visit us at www.eHarlequin.com

Printed in U.S.A.

ABOUT THE AUTHOR

Bestselling author Pamela Britton blames her zany sense of humor and wacky story ideas on the amount of Fruity Pebbles she consumes. Empowered by that Fruity Pebble milk, Pamela has garnered numerous awards for her writing, including a nomination for Best First Historical Romance by *Romantic Times*, a nomination for Romance Writers of America's Golden Heart, and the title of Best Paranormal Romance of 2000 by *Affaire de Coeur* magazine.

When not writing, Pamela enjoys showing her quarter horse, Strawflyin' Missile aka Peasy, and cheering on her professional rodeo cowboy husband, Michael. The two live on their West Coast ranch (aka Noah's Ark) along with their daughter, Codi, and a very loud, very obnoxious African Gray Parrot prone to telling her to "Shut up!"

Dear Reader,

Hey there, hidey-ho! My first book for Harlequin American Romance! Wow. Can you feel my excitement? For years I've written single-title historicals, always wondering what it'd be like to write modern-day stories. You have no idea how wonderful it was to use twenty-first-century slang like "You're joking" and "I swear," instead of "Surely you jest" and "'Pon my honor!"

I hope you enjoy *Cowboy Lessons,* the first of many— I hope—contemporary romances for Harlequin. The story was a blast to write, most especially since it takes place in a small town, something I happen to have a lot of experience with. Mixing that small town with a billionaire hunk who sweeps a local cowgirl off her feet was loads of fun. I hope you think so, too.

Incidentally, look for the sequel to *Cowboy Lessons* to arrive in bookstores sometime next year. Until then, feel free to drop me a line at www.pamelabritton.com. I give away cool prizes. Why? Because next to writing, shopping for my readers is my favorite thing to do (plus I get to write it off☺)!

Smiles and giggles,

Pamela

Chapter One

There were three truths in life, Scott Beringer decided. One, it didn't matter how wealthy or how famous you became: once a geek, always a geek.

Two, most geeks weren't very athletic.

Three, said computer geeks without said athletic ability had no business trying to ride a horse.

The last he knew from personal experience, because as sure as he could debug a software program, he was about to fall off the horse he was riding. That horse, a beast whose red hair should have given Scott his first inkling as to what kind of ride to expect, gave him a look of half disgust, half delight at finding a human being hanging half on, half off his left side. Scott tried to cling, he truly did. But no amount of butt clenching or leg flexing could save him. He had a brief thought as the ground approached from way up on high.

This is going to hurt.

It did.

Every bone in his body reverberated when he hit. Like a Saturday-morning cartoon character, he lay there, smooshed into the ground. Puffs of dirt drifted up on a warm breeze. A fly buzzed his face as if shocked to see him there. Through the whitewashed boards of the arena, he could see the face of the grizzled old cowboy who'd put him up on the horse.

He was doubled over. "Criminy," the old coot said, slapping his knee with laughter. "Did you see that? He looked like one of them rodeo trick riders."

Someone next to him nodded. Scott wasn't sure who.

"I reckon he's okay, though. Seems he's moving."

Scott—the human catapult—only groaned. He felt like a gnat who'd hit a front bumper at a hundred miles per hour. Sure, he was able to reach up and straighten his thick-framed black glasses, which had miraculously stuck to his head throughout the whole ordeal, but he'd be surprised if the eyes beneath those glasses weren't bulging.

A face loomed over him.

He opened his mouth, realized the wind was still knocked out of him, and gave up the idea of trying to greet the person, but, man, was she something.

Reddish-blond hair nearly the same color as the mane of the horse he'd fallen off of hung around her face in spunky little ringlets. As she frowned down at him, he noticed her wide, generous lips. And her eyes… They were the color of his computer monitor, a shade of blue he'd only ever seen created artificially. Those eyes stared down at him with concern and something else he couldn't quite identify.

"Mr. Beringer," she said. "If it's your intention to kill yourself here on the Lazy Y Ranch, you should let us know. It's easier to fit you with a body bag when you're alive."

Ah, a comedian.

He opened his mouth again, realized he still didn't have his breath back, and closed it.

"Are you hurt?" she asked, the look in her eyes turning to one of concern.

"No," he managed to say at last. "I'm fine," he added, because, hey, she was easily the prettiest woman he'd set eyes on in a long, long time, and he'd be damned if he'd act less than a man in front of her. What was it jocks said? Shake it off.

C'mon, Beringer, shake it off.

"Can you move?"

"Not if I don't have to."

"Here. Let me help you up." She held out a hand, and it was either a trick of the light or the pale blue denim shirt she wore that made those eyes of hers look almost green now. Wow. Long legs encased in jeans completed the picture, as well as cowboy boots that had definitely seen better days. He should know because he had a bird's eye view of those boots. They were right by his left eye.

"You sure I should move?" he asked, because, hey, he watched *ER* and knew you shouldn't move an accident victim.

She frowned. "Are you hurt that bad?"

"Only my pride."

"Can you move your legs and arms?"

"Do you have puppet strings 'cause I think that's the only way they'll work."

She immediately looked concerned again.

"Kidding. Kidding," he gasped, gasped because he tried to sit up to show her that he was a real man who could shake off a fall from a horse, and that he had faith in her if she thought he looked okay enough to move.

"Here." She offered her hand again.

He took it this time, everything within him stilling as his own large hand encased her slender fingers. He'd never thought of himself as having particularly large hands before, but he felt downright caveman-ish as he clasped hers.

"You okay?" she asked, spoiling the fantasy he'd had of dragging her off by the hair and out behind the barn, which only proved that he must have crowned himself harder than he thought, because he never had caveman thoughts about women he'd only just met.

He managed to sit up, put on his best game face, and say "I'm fine."

She tugged on his hand again, urging him to stand, which he did, reluctantly, the brand-new jeans and red-and-white-checkered shirt he wore coated in dirt.

"Are you sure you're all right?" she asked.

He kind of liked her concern for his well-being.

Frankly, it made him understand why cowboys did such stupid things like strap themselves to bulls and jump off horses mid-gallop. The sympathy factor obviously really worked. "Yeah. I'm fine."

She studied him a second longer, her wide mouth pressing into a thin line, her blue eyes narrowing just a tad before she said, "Good, then leave."

He thought he'd misheard her, even shook his head a bit to dispel the arena dust that must have plugged his ear canal. "I beg your pardon?"

"I said leave the ranch, Mr. Beringer."

The horse had stopped near the opposite end of the arena, Scott noticed, the man who'd mounted him on the beast—the former owner of the ranch—having caught the bronc. Obviously, the person who'd been standing next to him earlier had been her. Terrific. She'd seen his cannonball.

The woman with angry eyes crossed her arms. Scott was aware for the first time that she was tall. She had to be if she was shoulder level to his six-foot-three frame. "Leave," she repeated. "You low-down, dirty thief."

Thief? Uh-oh. Obviously she'd heard about the change of ownership of the ranch. "I didn't steal it."

"Not technically, but close enough."

"Buying property by paying the delinquent back taxes is perfectly legal."

"Legal, yes. Ethical, no. In my mind it's like foreclosing on a mortgage."

Well, put that way he could kind of see her point.
Kind of.

"You stole my father's land," she said, lifting her
hand and pushing her index finger into his chest. She
looked momentarily startled to find that it wasn't soft
flesh. Hah. Gym. Four days a week.

"And I aim to get it back," she finished, flexing
the finger she'd poked him with as if she'd hurt it.

Her father? "Look, it's not like I'm going to force
him from his house. As I told him earlier, I want him
to stay on."

She snorted, crossing her arms in front of her, that
pretty hair of hers flicked over one shoulder angrily.
"You couldn't force him out if you wanted to."

He almost pointed out to her that he really could,
if he wanted to. But the fact of the matter was, he
didn't. He'd acquired their ranch because of the in-
vestment value, but as he stared around him, he realized he truly liked the place. The two-story farmhouse looked charming with its wraparound porch.
An ancient-looking barn, turned a dusky gray, stood
not far from the arena, and multiple cross-fenced pastures stretched out behind it. It was hard to believe
they were less than an hour from the heart of California's Silicon Valley, and San Francisco's East Bay
was right over the hill.

"Another thing," she added, as if the laundry list
she'd pronounced wasn't enough. "You have no business riding a horse that isn't yours."

"But it is mine."

"You lying—" She struggled not to cuss. He could see that. "That horse belongs to my father."

"And I bought it from him."

"You *what?*"

For just a second Scott found himself studying her face. Anger set her whole cheeks aglow. Her ears were tipped in red. A spot on her brow, right above her nose wrinkled, delightfully. Even her small nose looked adorably red.

"Your dad sold it to me."

"My dad—" She looked momentarily speechless. "My dad sold you Rocket?"

Now it was Scott's turn to be surprised. "Is that his name?"

She nodded.

A new respect for the grizzled old cowboy who'd suckered him for two thousand dollars filled Scott. "He told me it was Buttercup."

She snorted again.

And then a new thought penetrated Scott's mind. "I could have been killed."

She gave him a look of mock sympathy. "I doubt you'd have been mourned for too long."

"Thanks," he said. Well, he supposed he couldn't blame her for being snippy. But still… He really had saved her father from being evicted, because he knew for a fact someone else had been right behind him ready to pay the tax bill. Literally. The guy had been at the window with him. But he decided not to argue the point.

"I really don't intend to turn your father out."

She didn't look in the least bit grateful for his intervention. As a matter of fact, she looked like that model he'd dated, right after he'd told her he thought she looked cute now that she'd gained some weight.

"You don't intend to turn him out," she said, shifting her weight onto one foot in a hip-jutting motion that Scott couldn't help but notice was really sexy. "Well, gee, Mr. Beringer, thanks ever so much. Considering this ranch has been in my family for three generations, that's very kind of you."

"Kindness is my middle name."

He'd been trying to make a joke. She didn't take it that way.

"Get out," she grated through teeth clenched like Thurston Howell's from *Gilligan's Island.* "Forget about the horse. I'll have my father mail you your money back."

"I can't do that."

"Why not?"

"Because it's kind of hard to be a cowboy without a horse."

AMANDA THOUGHT SHE'D misheard him. Frankly, she must have had the same expression on her face as he'd had when she'd told him to get off her father's land.

No, *his* land.

She fought back a hiss of anger. Why the heck her father had waited until today to tell her about the tax lien, she had no idea, but it was hard to say who she was more angry with: her father for not sharing the trouble the ranch was in, or Mr. Scott Beringer, Silicon Valley billionaire.

Oh, yeah, she knew who he was. She'd recognized him the moment she'd seen him at her feet. Her father's robber baron was none other than the reclusive boy wonder of the software industry.

"What do you mean, 'be a cowboy'?"

He smiled in a friendly sort of way, not that she had any intention of being that. "I want to learn to be a cowboy. Well, a rancher, really."

She digested the words for a second while she tried to come to grips with the fact that he really must be the nutcase the press made him out to be. A formidable nutcase, she reminded herself. Someone who did whatever it took to get what he wanted, at least if the newspapers were to be believed. But it was obviously true, because look how he'd acquired their land.

"Mr. Beringer, I think you've been inhaling too many silicon fumes."

He shrugged. Puffs of dust rose from his dirty red-and-white-checkered shirt. He looked ridiculous. Like a cross between Gene Autry and Buddy Holly with those thick-framed black glasses and wide green eyes. And yet…cute.

Ack. Where the heck had that thought come from?

"Why not? Maybe I need to take life a little less

seriously. Stop and smell the roses, if you will. Or the manure as the case may be.''

"So you looked around for a ranch to steal?''

"I didn't steal it. And, no, that's not why I did it. Frankly, it wasn't until this very moment that I realized I have a hankering to learn to ride the range.''

"Ride the range?''

"Sure. Herd cattle. Cook over a campfire. That sort of thing.''

"That sort of thing," she repeated because she really couldn't believe what she was hearing. "You think it's that easy?'' She snapped her fingers to illustrate. "Have you any idea how much work a ranch is?''

"So, then, if it doesn't work out, I'll sell the land back to you.''

For the second time, Amanda felt speechless. "You'll do what?''

"Sell it back to you.''

"Mr. Beringer—''

"Scott," he insisted.

Scott seemed like the wrong name for him. Attila. Genghis. Those seemed more appropriate.

"Scott," she said mildly, even though inside she felt as if she'd woken up in the middle of a *Saturday Night Live* skit. "My father is old. And he's been ill lately. Certainly not well enough to teach you the ropes.''

"Then *you* teach me.''

"Oh, no. No. No. No.'' She waved her hands and

shook her head, that mane of hair of hers bouncing around her shoulders.

"Sure, why not? I leave for Singapore tomorrow. We can start my horse lessons when I get back in a week."

"Horse lessons?"

"Yeah. I'll need to learn to ride my new horse."

He really must be insane.

And yet, what if he were serious? What if he really would give her the opportunity to buy the ranch back? Could she pass that up?

"No. I can't do it." And she wouldn't, no matter how tempting Beelzebub's offer. "I have a busy life, Mr. Beringer, and I don't have time to baby-sit." Although with the ranch gone, maybe she would.

"But I promise to be a good baby. No crying. No whining. And most important, no dirty diapers." He smiled a jack-o'-lantern grin.

But Amanda was impervious to his charms. "No."

He looked disappointed. He really did. "Well," he said, pulling a business card from his shirt pocket as if he'd expected to run into a fellow tycoon out here. Unbelievable. "If you change your mind, let me know."

She almost didn't take the card. Almost, but he waved it in front of her in a way that'd make it rude if she didn't. Besides, her father had always taught her to be polite. He was the new owner. She should be nice to him.

New owner.

Her hand clenched the card, twisting the paper.

He must have seen it because she thought she saw his face lose some of its spark. Well, too bad. She'd find another way to get the place back, that she vowed. She crossed her arms in front of her, telling him with her eyes that he should just leave.

They stared at each other for a full ten seconds before he finally said. "Okay. Well, then. I guess I'll be going."

"Well then, see you later."

"Bye."

But he still didn't leave right away. Instead he looked at her kind of strangely. As if he was memorizing her or something.

"Have a nice day," he said.

Have a nice day? Was he playing a scene from *Leave It to Beaver?*

She watched him turn and walk away.

Scott Beringer wanted to be a cowboy.

She *should* teach him how to be one. And make sure he hated every moment of it.

He climbed into a brand-new Mercedes, which, by the looks of it, probably cost more than all the back taxes he must have paid. The thought depressed her. How could they possibly hope to pay the man back?

"What'd he say?"

Amanda turned to her father, a man nearly as tall as she was, but who seemed to be shrinking daily. His blue eyes had gone rheumy in recent years, but they were still bright. Beneath a cap of gray hair his face looked red, though whether caused by drink or disappointment, she couldn't say. "He said you have a week to get out."

"He what?" Roy Johnson asked, straightening his stooped frame, the belly he'd had since before she could remember hanging over a tarnished belt buckle he'd won back in his rodeo days.

"Kidding, Dad. But it'd serve you right if he did."

Her father squinted his eyes at the departing car, his hands hooking into his leather belt. "He's younger than I thought he'd be."

"He wants cowboy lessons."

"Cowboy lessons?"

She eyed the man she loved more than any person on Earth. Her only family, and yet a man who'd managed to disappoint her more times in life than she cared to admit. She added today's fiasco to the list. "Yeah. Ranching lessons. Horse lessons. The whole bit."

"Are you going to teach him?"

"I told him to find someone else."

He blinked gray lashes, still staring at the car. "Humph. I wondered why he wanted to buy that horse."

"*That* horse could have killed him."

"Nah. He was safer than a tick on a deer."

She shook her head in disgust. She almost left it at that; experience told her that trying to make her dad accept responsibility for anything was a task best left alone. But she couldn't keep quiet.

"You should have told me what was going on, Dad."

"I never wanted this life for you, Amanda," he said, still not meeting her gaze. "You know that. It's why I sent you to that fancy college."

Fancy, in her dad's opinion, was anything away from the small town they lived in. Los Molina was fifty minutes from the Bay Area, but you'd never know it. Nestled in a small valley, the town enjoyed mild winters and cool summers. Perfect ranching country with rolling green hills and shady oaks.

"Dad, I happen to like this life."

"I think you could do better. Heck, I didn't let you go off to Cal Poly and get a degree in business agriculture so you could come home and use it."

"But I want to use that knowledge." Even though that hadn't always been the case. When she'd first realized she'd need to come home because of her father's failing health, she'd been bitterly disappointed. She'd wanted to use her degree to find her dream job: working for a thoroughbred breeding farm. Instead she'd been forced to come back home. But that was ancient history. She'd learned to love this place in the past few years.

"It's a hundred thousand dollars."

"What?"

"You asked me earlier how much I owed. One hundred thousand dollars."

She just about fell over. Lord, how the heck was she going to get the place back?

I want to learn to be a cowboy. The words bounced off the inside of her head as if she were in a drum. But she couldn't do it. She just couldn't.

Could she?

Chapter Two

She could. And a week later—a week during which she regretted agreeing to the ridiculous scheme the day after he'd proposed it—Amanda woke up to the *buwap-wap-wap-wap* of helicopter blades, which rattled her bedroom window and shook dust off her ceiling.

She knew immediately who it was.

"Give me a break," she muttered, tossing back the antique-ivory lace cover her grandmother had made almost seventy years ago. Leave it to Scott "Mr. Billionaire" Beringer to arrive in a helicopter.

She'd been dreading this day for a week, and so she took her time crawling out of bed. The hardwood floor felt cold beneath her bare feet as she crossed to the window and looked up. Sure enough, a white-and-black helicopter glided into view, the Global Dynamics logo visible against the gray-and-red sky of an early morning dawn. Pique made her jerk the lace curtains back as she moved to turn away, but just as quickly, she moved back to the window.

It looked like—

"No." She shook her head in disbelief. "No. Don't land in the bull pasture," she murmured. "Not the bulls."

But the spring grass in the pasture had already compressed from the pressure of the helicopter blades.

She turned around—the chilly morning air smacking her hard—then quickly pulled on rubber boots. Her blue-and-white-checkered flannel nightgown barely hung past her knees, but she paid it no attention as she squeaked along the hallway's hardwood floors…no, ran along the hallway.

"Not the bulls," she murmured again.

The outside morning air was cold enough to make her eyes water, the door swinging wide just in time for her to see the helicopter drop a passenger, then begin to lift off again.

"*Not* the *bulls*," she said, watching as Scott Beringer, wonder boy of the techno industry, did something incredibly stupid. He'd hopped out of the chopper into the middle of a field of bulls. Granted, they were cowering bulls right now. But not for long. Once that helicopter lifted off—

"Scott," she screamed. But she might as well have been yelling at her shadow. The chopper drowned out any sound: Scott calmly walked toward the wide gate as if he had all the time in the world, toting a black piece of luggage in one hand and a cowboy hat in the other. In the corner of the pen, one of her brown-and-white Herefords lowered its head. And as the helicopter began to lift, it became apparent that that particular bull would take it upon himself to be the sole representative of his species in stomping down the lone human intruder.

"Scott," she called again, panicked now.

The bull waited half a heartbeat before wringing its tail, a sure sign he was about to charge. He didn't have horns, but it wouldn't matter. When fifteen-hundred pounds of beef hit you broadside, you'd be lucky to walk away alive.

Oh, damn. She would succeed in killing him where her father had failed.

She waved her arms. Scott finally looked her way.

She pointed. Scott turned.

She yelled, "Run!"

And Scott Beringer, one of the wealthiest men in the United States, ran. Fast.

The suitcase got left behind, but not the hat. That he waved behind him as if shooing away a fly. Dumb, dumb, dumb. It only gained a bull's attention. But then the big Hereford spied the suitcase. It changed its path like Wile E. Coyote. Amanda never, not in a million years, would have thought a bull could turn that fast, but it did, heading toward the suitcase with its head down, tail flicking. The suitcase never stood a chance. It sailed through the air like a carnival ride. Scott, still running, looked back. The bull—its Samsonite enemy now vanquished—turned to Scott and put his head down again.

"Run," Amanda repeated. Not that he wasn't running already. Her blood thrust through her veins so fast it hurt her head. She began to wave her arms again, hoping to distract the bull. Didn't help. Scott's eyes looked panicked behind his thick glasses. "Stay." She thought she heard him yell. "Stay."

The bull charged. Scott wouldn't make it.

She arrived at the fence; Scott was about three feet away on the other side, three feet that he seemed to jump, launching himself like a Harlem Globetrotter.

The bull hurled himself at Scott, and maybe it reached him in time to help propel him, or maybe it was pure adrenaline that allowed Scott to cover so much ground, but he landed across the top rail and a second later, the bull hit the rail right below where he dangled. Scott was thrust off the top rail like a bird from a perch. He landed on his back and, as coincidence would have it, right at her feet. The hollow thud he made caused Amanda to wince, but she was so winded, and so relieved that he'd survived, all she could do was lean over and clasp her knees. "You lucky bastard."

The bull snorted its frustration from the other side of the fence.

"It attacked me," he protested.

She sucked in breaths of air.

"What is it with the animals on this ranch, anyway?"

Amanda ignored him, still huffing. "Go away,

Harry.'' She waved a hand at the bull, too winded to straighten just yet.

"Harry?" Scott said. "The thing's name is Harry?"

The bull turned, his muscles and veins enlarged, tail still ringing. When it caught sight of the suitcase again, it turned around, put its head down and charged.

A glance up revealed the helicopter still hovering above.

"Are you okay?" she finally decided to ask. Fact is, she felt a little angry. What kind of a fool tells his pilot to land in a field full of bulls?

Scott looked up at her, his arms straight out as if he were about to make a snow angel in the thick green grass he lay on. She noted he'd dressed differently, less like a character from a B movie and more like a real rancher. Denim shirt. Wranglers. His glasses—knocked from his head—lay near his right elbow, and his hair was spiked out around his head as if he'd been electrocuted. The hat had disappeared. She had a feeling it was beneath him. Smooshed.

"It chased me," he repeated.

Amanda waved at the pilot, telling him without words that Scott was fine. If he could complain, he was fine. The pilot waved back—she thought she saw him grinning beneath his insectlike goggles—then he angled the helicopter away and flew off.

Gradually, silence descended. Well, silence punctuated by her bull's goring of Scott's luggage. She had a feeling there wouldn't be many of his clothes left when all was said and done.

"I had no idea that thing would come after me with the helicopter hovering so near."

Man, her legs ached. And she had a side ache. And her damn feet ached.

"Lesson one, Mr. Beringer," she said as she slowly straightened. "A bull doesn't care if you're holding an Uzi or a flame thrower. When it's mad, it'll do whatever it wants."

Scott sat up on his elbows. "Uh-oh," he said.

Amanda's heart resumed it's double-time beat. "What? Is something broken?"

"I landed on something."

"Your hat," she theorized.

He winced. Concern turned into amusement when he leaned forward and she spied the crushed straw hat.

"Hope that wasn't new."

"It was," he grumbled, slowly coming to his feet as he smoothed his hair back. The hat lay on the ground like a discarded corn husk. Amanda was about to tell him that he didn't need it, but as she met his gaze, the words just sort of lodged in her throat.

Clark Kent looked good without his glasses. Very cute. And entirely too boyish to own a billion-dollar empire.

Lord, she couldn't imagine having a billion dollars.

One billion *dollars,* she repeated to herself like Dr. Evil.

"Are you hurt?" she asked again.

"Nothing but my pride." He repeated the same words as last week, and that had her remembering why he was here, and all of a sudden the depression returned with a vengeance. Even if she could convince him ranching wasn't his thing, how was she going to afford to pay him back? And if she couldn't pay him back, then what? Where would she go? Where would her father go? How many cattle ranchers would hire a woman, even if she did have a degree?

He tested a leg, then the other one, then moved his arms. The sound of her bull head-butting his suitcase faded. She looked up only to realize Harry had gotten the case open.

"Hey," Scott yelled, taking a step toward the rail, obviously not completely blind without his glasses.

"Forget it," Amanda advised, clutching his arm, only to immediately drop her hand. He had surprisingly large muscles. "If there's anything left, we'll pick it up later."

"What'll I use for clothes?"

"Why do you need clothes? You're not staying, are you?"

He looked up at her sharply, his glasses like a crooked hanger. "I told your father when I called last night that I'd be staying."

He'd called? And her father hadn't mentioned it?

Suddenly, the reason why her father had departed for parts unknown made sense. Typical Dad. Coward.

"He didn't tell me."

Scott's eyes slid over her. Amanda suddenly felt ridiculous, and self-conscious, even though the blue-and-white-checkered flannel gown couldn't be called revealing. Most of her lower legs were covered by her rubber boots, the kind with a wide red ring around the top, and they were mud-spattered and stained. She'd hardly noticed how beat-up they were. At least not before he took to staring at them.

"I'm going to kill him," she grumbled.

"Who?"

"My father."

"As long as it's not me."

"Tempting, but no."

SCOTT TOLD HIMSELF to be encouraged by that. She didn't want him dead, unlike her father. He looked past her to the house, wondering where the old coot had gotten to, but the moment his gaze rested on Amanda, his thoughts jammed like the keys of an old-fashioned typewriter. She looked even more adorable than he remembered.

You're losin' it, buddy, if you find a woman in black rubber boots sexy.

Odd thing, though: he did. "Hey, thanks for agreeing to do this. I'm really excited."

"Yeah, well, wait until your first day is over before getting too worked up."

Hmm. She was still sore over the loss of the ranch.

Well, he supposed he couldn't blame her. "Well, I'd still like to thank you, anyway."

"Let's get you cleaned up," she said by way of acceptance.

Well, the apology thing didn't work.

She turned away without a backward glance, saying, "Follow me."

He did, stepping in behind her. The back of her was even more charming than the front. He wasn't usually a body-parts man. That he left to beer-swilling football fanatics. But he found himself liking Amanda Johnson's parts. Rounded bottom, shapely legs, at least what he could see above the boots. Nice smell, too, even this early in the morning. It wafted back to him on the early morning breeze. Natural. Earthy and yet wholly feminine in a way that most of the women he'd dated had never been.

The house she led him toward was a one-story rectangle with a wide wraparound porch, old-fashioned windows with real wood frames and five creaking steps that led to the front door. To the left of the house was a large brown barn with big brown double doors. To the right was another barn—brown, too—this one a single-story affair that had doors off the back that opened into individual pens. Horse pens. And he would bet there were four more matching doors and pens on the other side. A horse barn—though it looked ancient and not at all like the fancy affairs one could see off of I-280 when he drove around Silicon Valley.

"I feel like I'm on the set of *Bonanza.*"

"Yeah, well, welcome to my home, Little Scott."

"Hey, you watched *Bonanza,* too?"

"Yeah."

Her answer sounded more like "What of it?" and Scott tried not to feel wounded. "Where's your dad?"

"Away, apparently." And the way she said *that* didn't invite more small talk.

She held a heavy oak door open and stepped aside. She smelled even nicer close up. Better than him, probably, after his trek through cow poop.

The inside of the home was cozy. Surprisingly high ceilings. What looked to be bedrooms to his right, kitchen and family room to his left. She paused just inside the door and—holy moley—bent over to tug off her boots. Slowly, like a stripper. Not that he'd seen many strippers wearing rubber boots…or any strippers, period. But he imagined one would take off rubber boots slowly like she did, exposing one inch of flesh at a time.

Unbelievable. Who would have thought the sight of her slipping off latex boots would be sexy? But darned if it wasn't.

She glanced up just then—saw that he was staring at her legs—and straightened abruptly.

A voice inside his head said, *uh-oh.*

"I'll go find you a clean shirt."

Scott was not a stupid man. He realized ogling a woman who would be responsible for his safe-keeping in the coming week was likely not a wise thing to do. She looked as if she was fighting to hold on to her temper.

"Thanks."

She pressed her lips together before she turned on her now bare—and might he add, adorable—feet to head back toward the bedrooms. She had nice ankles, he realized. Petite yet sturdy.

Sturdy?

What was she, a cow? And yet like a herd animal himself, he suddenly found himself following her. A bull. He was Ferdinand the Bull.

She turned. Their bodies connected. She jerked back, her hand splaying on his chest. "What are you doing?"

"Following you."

"Don't do that. I'll bring you the shirt."

"Where will I change? After all, I wouldn't want you going all mushy on me when you catch sight of my hard body."

Did she blush? Did she actually blush? Incredible.

"You want to get the shirt, fine. My father's room is at the end of the hall. I'm going to get dressed."

She would get dressed...

Her arms lifting her nightgown, her breasts revealed. Skin so smooth it looked like wedding satin exposed to his flesh....

"Mr. Beringer?"

He started.

"Did you hear me?"

He felt his own cheeks fill with color. Amazing. Now *he* was blushing.

"Yeah. That's fine."

She stared up at him with narrowed eyes. "If you want to wash up, you can use the bathroom attached to my father's bedroom."

For a second his imagination twisted the words into an invitation to share the shower with her.

In your dreams, Scott.

"Be careful because the tap water gets hot fast." She kept her gaze on him for a second longer, as if she was worried he might still follow her.

"Thanks."

She gave him one last look before turning away. Wow. What was it about her that had him thinking such testosterone-charged thoughts? That had him wondering what kind of man she was attracted to? That had him wishing it was his kind of man.

You're not her type, Scott old man.

No, but he could dream, couldn't he?

Just one night in bed with her. That's all he wanted. He wasn't fool enough to believe anything more than that could last. It never did.

It took him only a second to find the room in question, and the shirt, and then he began to wash up and change. By the time he'd finished, he heard her running a shower. That shot a new burst of energy through him. Amanda Johnson naked. That must be a sight. She'd be tanned. He wondered if it was an all-over tan.

Scott, you're losing it.

He was, but he'd known that before arriving. During the week he'd been away he'd found himself thinking of her constantly. During the long, long flight back from Singapore he'd wondered if he'd feel the same way when he saw her again. Despite having embarrassed himself in front of her again, he did.

Distraction. He needed a distraction. The kitchen. Only a handful of people knew that he loved to cook. Hell, he was a better-than-average cook. He was a great cook. Scott had long since figured out that his love of food probably had something to do with his lack of it as a child. But whatever the reason, he prided himself on his hidden talent.

She was in the shower alone.

Stop it, Scott.

Five minutes later he'd found pans, spices and various other items he might need. The appliances were ancient, but the place had a homey feeling to it. Chickens ran around the wallpaper, the curtains and the small rug in front of the sink. He'd even found an apron in the shape of a giant chicken in the drawer, the wings spreading back to tie around his waist. He put it on without a moment's hesitation, then opened the refrigerator door in preparation for a raid.

''What are you doing?''

Scott turned, startled to see a wet-haired Amanda standing in the doorway. What'd she do, jump in and out?

You'll need a cold shower if you keep reacting to her in this way.

Darn, but if he'd thought her pretty with that cascade of hair falling loose around her shoulders, she was even prettier with it slicked back.

"I'm going to cook you breakfast."

"I don't eat breakfast."

Something inside Scott fizzled like a spent firecracker. "You don't?"

She shook her head.

He told himself not to be disappointed. *Regroup, Scott.* No big deal. She likely wouldn't have been impressed by his cooking skills, anyway. "Ah, but you've never had one of my breakfasts."

Her pretty blue eyes looked large and luminous without her hair framing her face. "Mr. Beringer."

"Scott," he instantly corrected.

"Scott," she said. "A rancher usually feeds the livestock before he feeds himself."

"Really?"

She nodded.

"But I thought we were the dominant predators."

"The what?"

"We eat when we want to eat. They eat when we want them to eat."

She shook her head. "They get mad when they're made to wait. And you saw what happens when a bull gets angry."

His suitcase. He'd forgotten about it.

"But I was going to make you my special huevos rancheros in honor of my first day on the homestead."

Her eyes narrowed—it must have been the word *homestead*. It didn't take a man with a doctorate in computer science to figure out that she was thinking it was no longer *her* homestead.

"Do you want to learn about ranching or not?"

"Of course I do."

"Then let's go."

"Not until we eat. You know, breakfast is the most important meal of the day."

"Fine. *I'll* go feed the livestock."

He closed the refrigerator door. "No, wait. I'll go with you."

She didn't look relieved. In fact, she looked kind of irritated. "Hey, slow down," he called.

"The steers are hungry, Mr. Beringer. I don't like to make them wait."

"And here I thought ranchers ate hearty breakfasts."

"You're not a rancher, Mr. Beringer." And her unspoken words were that he'd never be.

Scott stiffened, and if she'd known him better she would have realized her mistake. One never, ever challenged Scott Beringer...not if they hoped to win.

Chapter Three

Amanda felt Scott staring at her all the way out to the barn doors.

Had she been too hard on him? Should she care if she had been?

No, she firmly told herself. The whole week she'd waited for his return, she'd thought of ways to scare him off. The first of those plans started right now.

And yet she felt a surprising stab of guilt, and the urge to banter around with him. Ridiculous. The man had stolen her family's heritage. He was like one of those cattle tycoons of the old days, the ones that squatted on small rancher's land. His picture should be inserted into dictionaries under the words *robber baron*.

I'm going to cook you breakfast.

She'd *wanted* to eat breakfast with him.

Careful, Amanda. You might find yourself actually liking him.

She pulled open the giant wood doors that exposed

the interior of the barn to early morning sunlight. Dust motes flew through the air on streamers of sunlight that illuminated a wall of hay.

"Wow," Scott said. "That's a lot of bricks."

Bricks? She almost laughed.

"They're called bales," she corrected. "And there're twenty tons of them."

"Twenty *tons?*"

She nodded. "And we'll go through most of it by the end of next month."

"But I thought cattle grazed on grass."

She turned to him. Her hair had dried a bit, despite the chilly morning air. She wore a gray sweater that she realized now was the wrong thing to wear. Slivers of the hay would stick to it and prick her all day. Darn. She hadn't been thinking clearly.

"Cattle need at least ten acres of pasture grass per head. That means we'd need approximately ten thousand acres for all the cattle we have. Since the ranch is less than two hundred acres, and we're able to lease only a few hundred more, we have to supplement with rice hay."

"Rice hay?"

"It's cheaper than grass, and cattle do well on it."

"So what the hay?" he joked.

She caught the smile that almost slipped out at the last moment, going to the right and pulling down two sharp metal hooks before turning back to him.

"Planning on dressing as Captain Hook for Halloween?"

"No," she said. "You are."

"I are what?"

"Going to be Captain Hook." She handed him the hay hooks. "Here you go," she said with a bright smile. "You need to load a ton of it into the back of our one-ton."

"I *what?*"

She really shouldn't feel bad about the look on his face. She shouldn't. But it was hard not to feel just a little bit guilty at the expression of horror he shot her.

"A ton of it," she reiterated. "That's about twenty-five bales."

"You've got to be kidding."

She shook her head, having to fight back the smile again. "No, I'm not." She refrained from telling him that she usually helped her father load the bales. It was easier with two people. Instead she said, "If you want to be a rancher, this is one of the chores you'll have to do. Daily."

"Daily?"

Now he looked horrified. Poor guy. Poor *what*? Now wasn't the time to start feeling sorry for him. "What's the matter? Not up to the task? 'Cause if you're not, we can certainly stop right now. Of course, you'll have to give up on your plan to become a cowboy."

His eyes narrowed. And once again that odd transformation came over him, the one she noted the first day they'd met. Like the chameleon she'd seen in the local pet store he changed right before her eyes. He seemed to stand straighter, the intelligence that always shone from his eyes intensifying until it made her feel distinctly uncomfortable. This was the man who'd formed a software company from the ground up. Who was worth more money than she would ever see in an entire lifetime. Who did not, if the press was to be believed, take no for an answer.

"I'll do it."

"Great," she said. But she really didn't think he'd make it past five bales. Okay, maybe seven. "I'll wait here while you go get the truck."

He gazed at her a moment longer, something within Amanda stilling at that look. She was almost relieved when he turned away, set the hooks on one of the lower bales, then headed out of the barn.

"Keys are in it."

He lifted a hand in silent acknowledgment but didn't glance back. Less than five minutes later, he was backing the diesel into the barn in a manner that made Amanda wonder if he'd driven big vehicles before. She'd expected him to have to struggle to fit the wide truck through the double doors, but he cruised on in as if he'd done it a hundred times.

That was her first surprise.

Her second came when he turned off the loud motor, the smell of diesel making her wave her hand in front of her face and cough. The dust motes were in action again, tickling the inside of her nose. A dove nesting in the barn's rafters coo-cooed into the sudden silence. Scott hopped out of the truck, reached up and removed his glasses only to drop them into his pocket, then went to the tailgate. It lowered with a thud. Next, he picked up the hay hooks, one in each hand, turned to the nearest golden bale and sunk the hooks with a *thunk* that belied an ease Amanda would have never thought possible. He lifted the one-hundred-and-twenty-pound bale, saying, "How do I stack it?" and sounding not at all out of breath as he did so.

She was so surprised, she found herself saying, "Put it all the way in the front, up against the back window, long side against the bed," before she remembered she'd wanted him to figure that out on his own.

He nodded, hefting the bale inside without even huffing, then climbing inside to position it correctly. And now that she thought about it, he hadn't sounded at all out of breath after his running of the bulls this morning. In fact, he'd sounded in better shape than she.

He jumped down from the back of the truck, his legs flexing expertly as he landed. Amanda stepped back and crossed her arms in front of her.

The next one went in just as easily.

So did the next.

And the next.

He was sweating a bit by the time he'd loaded seven. The next five went in a bit more slowly, but that was because he had to lift the bales atop the others. By the time he hit twenty, he'd figured out on his own the best way to stair-step them on top of one another.

Amanda didn't say a word.

Ten minutes later he was done. A little winded and a bit sweaty, but done. He turned to her and said, "Now what?"

Amanda had to close her mouth.

Maybe it was the he-man way he'd loaded the hay. Maybe it was the way he so casually leaned against the tailgate of the truck. Or maybe it was because he suddenly didn't look a thing like a computer genius. Whatever it was, she had to struggle to remember his question.

Hubba, hubba, what a man.

Hubba, hubba…have you lost your mind?

"Now what?" she repeated to herself. She stiffened. "Er, ah. Now you go out to the pasture and feed them."

"The bulls?"

"No, no…they have enough to graze on. The hundred heads of steers next to the bulls."

"All right." He came toward her. And suddenly Amanda went on heightened alert. If she was a submarine, her red lights would be blinking. He stopped right in front of her.

Warning. Warning. Warning.

"You have some dust on your face."

Dust?

"It probably dropped from the barn roof," she said, her voice seeming to come from a distance.

"Do you want me to remove it?"

"Sure," she said, before she recalled the way she'd felt when they'd bumped into each other in the house, the way she felt right now, because there could be no denying the way her whole body buzzed as he came near, the way the look in his eyes made her stare up at him unblinkingly, the way she felt as he lifted a hand, then gently, oh so gently wiped the dust away from her cheek.

"There," he said.

And, oh, my, she couldn't believe it, but just that touch made her grow damp between the legs.

She was attracted to Scott Beringer.

Get a grip, Amanda.

She felt dizzy, realized it was because she was holding her breath, then sucked in a blast of oxygen. That helped. Marginally. "How—" She had to work her mouth in order to make the words come out. "How do you see without your glasses?"

"I don't need my glasses for anything but reading. In fact, I'll just move them to the truck, if you don't mind."

Mind? Mind what? Oh, yeah. The glasses. "No. That's fine."

He smiled. Amanda just about melted. It was a crooked smile. Not suave. Not flirtatious, just a genuine crooked smile that made her heart all but melt at the boyish, yet masculine friendliness of it.

She stepped back, waved a hand at her face, saying, "Dust," in case he thought she was doing something silly, like waving the heat out of her cheeks, which she was.

Lord, you've got the hots for Scott Beringer.

There were a million reasons why that shouldn't be, not the least of which was that he'd stolen their land. And yet she couldn't deny the truth, despite what she tried to tell herself.

"Um, if you don't mind, I'm going to let you do the feeding part all by yourself."

"By myself?"

She nodded and said, "It's easy." And it was. "You just drive about two hundred yards out and start feeding. Honk the horn when you're done." She turned away from him before he realized the reason why she wouldn't meet his gaze was because she was in danger of doing something silly, like touch him. Or maybe even jerk his head down and kiss him.

"Where are you going?" he called after her.

"Into the house to make breakfast."

"But I'll do that."

Oh, no, he wouldn't, because just right now she didn't need to admire him any more than she did, and she had a feeling Scott would cook as well as he did everything else.

"I'll cook," she said over her shoulder, nearly running into the door in the process.

Get a hold of yourself, Amanda.

"You just remember to close the gate when you're done."

She didn't know if he nodded or not, didn't know

because she was halfway across the barnyard before she heard the truck start up.

Breakfast first, then part two of her plan. She could handle that, right?

Right?

Chapter Four

It was a sign of how discombobulated she was that it took her nearly a half hour to realize something was wrong. Very wrong.

By Amanda's calculations, it should have taken Scott roughly twenty minutes to feed the steers, and that was taking into consideration his inexperience. But when the clock struck a quarter hour, Amanda figured she'd better check on him. Turning off the stove, Amanda removed a pot of sizzling sausages, their basil-and-garlic smell making her stomach growl.

What had he done?

She saw for herself a few seconds later.

Scott Beringer sat in the back of the truck atop a bale, only when he saw her, he shot up like a patio umbrella. Surrounding him on the ground were bales of hay, unopened, frustrated cattle milling around as they tried to get to the food. Scott tried to shoo them away so he could jump down, but he was simply outnumbered and likely too afraid to plunge into the midst of a hundred head of cattle.

She heard his faint cry of help.

"Well, I'll be," she murmured.

Why the heck hadn't he opened the bales?

Because you didn't tell him to.

She slapped her forehead. "You idiot," she yelled, but it was hard to say who she meant, her or Scott.

She'd have to go rescue him.

SCOTT COULDN'T BELIEVE how relieved he was to see Amanda Johnson riding her horse toward him. Granted, it was usually the man that rescued the woman, but beggars couldn't be choosers. Besides, this particular knight looked great atop a horse—better than he would. Her hair had dried into its masses of ringlets, the breeze picking up a red strand and playing with it. She looked glorious with the morning sky as a backdrop, and all he wanted to do was touch her. Unfortunately, she didn't look half as impressed with him as he was with *her*.

"Nice going," she said as she pulled her horse to a stop just outside the herd of cattle.

"I'd only fed a few bales and suddenly I was surrounded."

"You're supposed to open them first."

"Open them?"

She shook her head, and he wasn't sure, but he was pretty certain she rolled her eyes, too. But then she kicked her horse forward, and the cattle parted as if her horse were a bowling ball and the cattle the pins.

"If you wrap the hay hooks around the twine," she said as she got close enough for him to see that her waist was tiny when tucked into jeans, "it'll snap the cord. You throw flakes to the steers, not the whole bale."

"You didn't tell me that."

"No, I didn't," she admitted with a total honesty that took him by surprise. "My mistake."

This woman was apologizing? Was the sky falling?

"Here," she said. "Climb aboard. We'll let them eat what they can and then come back to move the truck later."

He'd like to climb on top of her.

But, of course, that would never happen. Not at his present rate of impressing her.

She held the horse in place while he slipped a leg over, then settled behind her with an ease that took him by surprise. But the moment his front made contact with her back, he grew instantly hard. Darn, she turned him on. Maybe it was the whole country girl thing, but suddenly he wondered if she'd look good in gingham and pearls.

"Wrap your arms around my waist."

For real? She wanted him to touch her? He didn't hesitate.

"Now, hold on."

He held on, pulling her up against the front of his

chest. Darn. She may have a hard body, but she was all woman beneath.

"Haven't you ever watched a western before?" she asked, tilting her head a bit to stare at him out of the corner of her eye.

It took a moment for her words to penetrate the lust-induced haze he'd sunk into. And even then, he still couldn't follow what she meant.

She must have seen his confusion. "Didn't you ever wonder where those little flakes of hay came from?"

He had to force himself to swallow before saying, "Sure I've watched westerns, but I never paid close enough attention to them to know those little bricks open up."

"Bales," she mumbled, and he could have sworn he heard laughter in her voice. "They're called bales."

Good thing the back of her saddle separated their lower extremities, otherwise she'd figure out fast that the only hay he was thinking about was the hay he wanted to roll her in.

"I'm not off to a very good start, am I?"

He felt her stiffen, felt her kind of jerk a bit before saying, "Actually, you're not doing too bad."

They were the first kind words he'd had from her, and they made Scott's heart pitter-patter.

"Yeah, well," he croaked before coughing to dispel the odd crick in his throat. "I've decided to hire someone to do the feeding."

She was silent a long moment. The horse swayed beneath them. The smell of leather rose up to mingle with her scent. Lemons. She smelled like a giant lemon, and he liked it.

"It must be nice," she said.

"What?"

"To be able to buy whatever you want."

"It is."

She turned quiet after that. That was fine, Scott was too busy wondering if she'd mind taking a turn around the pasture. It was a beautiful morning. Very *Sound of Music*. Off in the distance a chicken clucked. Behind them steers mooed. All he needed was a pair of chaps, some pistols and a rope. And Amanda. John Wayne always got the girl.

"When I was in high school I had it in my head that I wanted to be the National High School Rodeo Association champion barrel racer," she broke the silence by saying. "We had a horse that my dad picked up at auction. He was short, but man was he fast."

She paused before the gate, but she didn't move to open it. The horse shifted beneath them, but she seemed lost in another world. "At the beginning of my senior year nobody could touch us, and this girl, Andrea Thomas was her name, must have gotten sick of it because her dad showed up at our house one day. I didn't know what he wanted, didn't ask, just watched him go into the house to talk to my dad." She paused, shaking her head a bit, a strand of her hair tickling his face. "You want to know what he wanted?"

He nodded, even though he had a feeling where she was going with this.

"He wanted to buy my horse, only, see, it wasn't my horse. It was my dad's. He'd bought it and I guess he felt he had a right to sell it." He felt her whole body tense just before she said, "He did."

If Scott had thought her father a total loser before, he was even more of a loser now. "He didn't."

She nodded. "For a bunch of money. Oh, he gave me some of it…to buy myself a new horse he said, as if the hours I'd spent on Thumper's back could be bought back." She shook her head again. "I've spent as many hours—more, actually—running this ranch, tending to the cattle, breeding them, selling them, and once again my father went and sold it from under me. Well, not sold, just lost it, which in some ways is even worse." She tilted her head, and for the first time there was no animosity in her eyes as she said, "If you go back on your word to sell this place back to me if ranching isn't your thing, Mr. Beringer, I promise I'll buy the best hit man I can afford. You have my word on that."

At that moment, he almost offered to sell the place back to her. Right then and there. But he couldn't bring himself to do it. Not when it'd always been a dream of his to own a ranch—a real ranch—like this. But if he decided to keep the place, maybe he could work something out with her. He might not be able to give her Thumper back, but he could give her the next best thing.

"Don't move," she said.

Scott was about to ask why, but she threw a leg over the front of her saddle and slipped from his arms before he could say a word.

She didn't get back on, either, just led him through the gate like a child on a pony ride. And she never looked up at him, either. He suspected it was because she didn't want him to see what was in her eyes. But he knew. Yes, he knew. Right after his parents had died, he'd watched as the State had sold all their personal belongings before placing him in foster care. He'd only been allowed to pack up one box. Granted, he'd never had a lot of toys, but he still remembered the hurt at having to leave some of them behind.

"Let me down."

She must not have heard him at first because she kept leading the horse.

"Amanda, I need to get down. Now."

She stopped then, the horse doing the same. When she looked up at him, Scott saw himself in her eyes.

"What's wrong?" she asked.

He didn't answer, just mimicked what she'd done a few minutes before. He almost fell flat on his face but clutched at the foot-strap thingies when he landed, which saved him—stirrups, they were called.

"What is it?" she repeated as he closed the distance between them.

Scott lifted her chin. "I'd buy you ten Thumpers if I could."

He saw her eyes widen, that gaze a splendid mix of blues and greens and grays. Then she blinked and swallowed at the same time. It took him a moment to realize that it was because she'd teared up. Ah, hell.

He kissed her.

He'd wanted to do it all morning, and he wasn't sorry that he did so now. He expected peaches and cream. He got a Fourth of July firecracker, right down to the sparks.

She gasped in surprise. So did he. But then he was slipping his tongue inside her mouth, tasting her. Wanting her. Lapping her up.

And she kissed him back. She didn't protest. Didn't jerk away from him. She seemed to feel the instant *kapow* that he did.

Her hands came up to his head, her fingers entwining the hair at his nape. His hands explored her sides, a part of him calculating the risk it would be to move his hand up and cup a breast...or two. Man, how he wanted that. But he couldn't.

Instead he forced himself to draw back. One of his hands lifted to cup her chin again. Her eyes were closed. Freckles dusted her nose, her lashes long against her tanned cheeks.

Then her eyes suddenly sprang open and she looked a tad bit freaked, so he said, "I hope you don't mind my doing that, but you seemed like you needed something to turn your mind from Thumper."

She stiffened in his arms. "Scott—"

"No," he said. "Don't say a word. You needed a kiss. Don't make more of it than it is."

She didn't look like she believed him. He didn't blame her. He didn't believe himself.

"Thank you," she said.

A second later she turned toward the house. And Scott just stood there, arms hanging limply at his sides, wondering why it was he felt so weird.

It was only when he realized she'd left her horse behind that Scott realized he wasn't the only one thrown.

Chapter Five

The thing about living in a small town, Amanda thought, as she came to a halt not three seconds after turning away from Scott, was that everybody knew your business before you did. Amanda would bet if her house caught on fire, her neighbors would be the ones to call 911.

Such was the case now, for as sure as she wore a C-cup, that was Stephanie Prichart coming up her drive.

Not now, Amanda thought. Not when she was still trying to come to grips with the fact that Scott Beringer had kissed her, and she'd *liked* it. Not when her heart had melted at his "I'd buy you ten Thumpers" comment. Not when all she wanted to do was escape to the house and try to figure out just what it was about the man that seemed to get under her skin.

But there was no mistaking the green Camry pulling to a halt before her house. Nor the wide smile on the face of the blond driver.

Amanda tried not to groan.

There wasn't anything *wrong* with Stephanie. Amanda had known her since Fisher-Price days. It was just that Stephanie was so…so Carol Brady. Perpetually happy, always giggling—not laughing, but giggling—she was the type of person that you liked, but that you had a hard time tolerating sometimes. Like now. This morning, to be exact, because Amanda knew the moment Stephanie opened her car door that she'd somehow found out about Scott's presence.

Well, Amanda supposed it was hard to miss a helicopter.

"Darn," she said as the door opened.

"Amanda," Stephanie trilled. As clichéd as it was, *trilled* was the only word one could use to describe the way Stephanie spoke. Like Snow White sucking some serious helium.

"Amanda, you naughty girl. Why didn't you tell me you had a houseguest?" Stephanie looked toward Scott as if his presence was a complete surprise. *Hah.*

Blond, petite, entirely too Silicon Valley to suit Amanda's taste, Stephanie approached, her overbleached teeth smiling as her designer boots sounded as if they were munching the gravel drive. *Cruncha, cruncha, cruncha.*

"Stephanie, how nice to see you, too." It wasn't really, not now, but Amanda managed to smile. Though she wished she hadn't because smiling pulled the skin tight around her lips, which were overly sensitive thanks to Scott's kiss.

Stephanie had a close-up view of that skin because she came forward and gave her a hug. That was the thing about Stephanie, no matter how nosy and annoying she was, you just had to love her. She gave the best darn hugs.

"Why haven't you been by to visit?" she asked upon drawing back, her green eyes darting from Amanda's eyes, to Scott, then back again.

"Oh, you know. So many men, so little time."

Stephanie lifted her brow, looking back at Scott.

"I meant bulls, Stephanie, not human men."

Stephanie giggled. Amanda tried not to wince.

"Who's this?"

Amanda didn't want to do it. She really didn't, but she had no choice but to turn back to Scott, who was holding the reins of the horse she'd abandoned, and said, "Stephanie, this is Scott Beringer."

Of course, Stephanie had likely already known that. There'd probably been a APB put out the moment his helicopter had landed. See, that was the thing. Everyone knew everyone's business, but the trick was to act as if you didn't know the other person's business.

Stephanie echoed, "Scott Beringer," in a gushing voice. "*The* Scott Beringer?"

"Yes, Stephanie," Amanda said. "*The* Scott Beringer." And something about the way Stephanie stared at Scott, as if he were God's gift to Stephanie's pet charities—of which there were many—made

Amanda say, "You know, corporate raider. Company downsizer. Robber baron." Which made Scott and Stephanie both swing their gazes around to her, Scott going so far as to lift his brows. Amanda felt her face color like a barbecue with lighter fluid squirted on top.

"Just kidding," she said, because it wasn't like her to be so mean spirited. Man, he'd really rattled her with his kiss.

Stephanie, however, was oblivious to the sexual undercurrents going around. "It's so nice to meet you, Mr. Beringer," she said. "I've heard so many wonderful things about you."

Which made Amanda's own brows lift. She had? From whom?

"Amanda, you should have told me Mr. Beringer was a personal friend of yours."

Personal friend? *Hah.* As if. But Amanda didn't contradict her, because if there was a chance Stephanie didn't know about Scott stealing her father's ranch out from under them, Amanda wasn't going to enlighten her.

Then Scott came forward, or at least he tried to. He didn't know anything about horses, Amanda suddenly recalled, because he walked forward as if Fancy—the horse Amanda had abandoned in her kissed-senseless daze—would automatically follow, which she didn't, and Scott got jerked back to the point he almost fell backward when the reins grew taut.

He recovered quickly, stopping, shooting Fancy a dogmeat look before smiling at Stephanie and saying, "Nice to meet you, Ms. Prichart."

"Oh, it's Stephanie," she trilled. "Call me Stephanie."

"And you can call me Scott."

"Scott," Stephanie corrected, the two smiling at each other as if they were members of a mutual admiration society.

"Did you want to come inside, Stephanie?" Amanda asked. "I was just about to make breakfast."

"Are you in town to escort Amanda to the barn dance tomorrow night?" Stephanie asked as if she hadn't heard her. But Amanda knew she had. What was more, Amanda knew the question was a ploy to lead the conversation toward said barn dance.

"Stephanie, no—"

"Barn dance?" Scott asked, his brows lifting again.

Amanda almost groaned. She almost grabbed the well-meaning Stephanie by the arm and dragged her inside. But she couldn't. Not without being a wee bit obvious. And not without Scott realizing she didn't want Stephanie to talk about the barn dance, which in turn meant Scott knowing about it. Which in turn would indicate that she was scared he'd come to it. Which would make her seem a coward—

"Yeah," Stephanie said brightly. "A barn dance. It's tomorrow, at the Los Molina Hall. Everyone's invited. The whole town usually comes, even the kids.''

''Stephanie, I'm sure Scott doesn't want to go to our little get-together.''

''Actually, I do.''

Which made Amanda groan. Inwardly, of course.

''Great,'' Stephanie said. ''There's a silent auction. And it's a potluck, but I'm sure Amanda was planning to bring something, weren't you, Amanda.''

''Actually, I'm not sure I can go—''

''Of course you can, Amanda. Why you just told me last night that you were going. Don't tell me you changed your mind because you have a houseguest; not when he can come, too.''

Scott had to admit, Amanda didn't look like she wanted to go, but she would. He'd make sure of it. Heck, he'd never been to a barn dance before. He'd never been to any kind of dance. Well, he'd gone to charity balls, but not with any kind of date. This would be a first for him, even if his ''date'' didn't look too terribly enthusiastic about the whole thing.

''What time does it start?'' he asked Amanda's friend.

''At eight.''

He nodded. ''We'll be there.''

''Terrific.'' Stephanie turned to Amanda. ''You and I can catch up then.''

''Great,'' Amanda said, but in a tone of voice that indicated she thought it was anything but great.

Stephanie didn't seem to notice. Instead she smiled

brightly, turned and headed back to her car. She paused by the door, her blond hair swishing over one shoulder as she said, "Nice meeting you, Scott."

"You, too," he said, raising a hand.

She got in, the car door popping closed, while Scott and Amanda stood side by side as Stephanie started the car and drove off.

"We're not going," Amanda said the minute Stephanie drove away.

"Oh, yes, we are."

"No, we're not," Amanda said, turning to him.

It was time, Scott realized, that Amanda realized he was no pushover, that he made a habit out of going after what he wanted. And what he wanted, he suddenly realized, was Amanda.

"We're going, Amanda, because if we don't go, there's not a chance in hell that I'll sell this place back to you."

Her mouth dropped open, those sexy lips of hers still red from their kiss.

Don't make more of it than it is, he'd said. But he intended to make more of it. A lot more.

"Why, you blackmailing fiend."

"Fiend?" he couldn't help but say on a laugh. "I don't think I've ever been called a fiend before."

"Jerk. Butthead. Either of those ring a bell?" She crossed her arms in front of her, her jaw stiffening as she glared up at him.

"No, but there's always a first."

To which she said nothing, continuing to glower,

the horse he held the reins to chomp-chomp-chomping at the bit, as if angry, too.

"Why?" she suddenly asked. "Why do you want to take me to a barn dance? Have you any idea how silly they are? They square dance. Have you ever seen people square dance?"

"On *Hee Haw* once or twice."

"*Hee Haw?* You've watched *Hee Haw?*"

"One of my foster parents loved it."

That made her stiffen, made her look at him with sudden intensity. "Foster parents?" she asked with a tilt of her head.

It was more than he'd intended to reveal, but after her Thumper story, he supposed he owed her a little honesty, too. "When my folks died, I was sent to live with foster parents."

"You were?"

He nodded. "Actually, I had a lot of foster parents. The State was always moving me around. That's the thing about foster care, you could never get too attached to your guardians because the next week, they may not be your guardians anymore."

He'd expected her to react with surprise. To maybe call him a butthead again and go back to arguing about the dance. Instead she tilted her head in an oddly endearing way.

"I'm sorry," she said. "I lost my mother in a riding accident. Worst day of my life. I can't imagine losing both parents."

"Riding accident?"

"A colt reared up, she slipped back, and when the horse fell, the saddle horn caught her in the chest. She died instantly."

But there was something in her eyes, something that made him say, "You saw it happen, didn't you?"

He saw her eyes widen a bit just before she looked away. "I did."

His heart did something odd then. It hurt in an almost physical way, her pain becoming his, her heartache shared.

"I'm sorry."

She shrugged. "Dad took it hard." She met his gaze then. "He drowned his sorrows in a bottle. Literally. I threw myself into schoolwork, got a scholarship, earned a degree in business agriculture."

She'd learned to live without her mother, Scott finished for her, much as he'd learned to live without his parents, but one never forgot a parent. There were all those reminders. Mother's Day. Father's Day. Birthdays. Not to mention the times it would come upon you suddenly, the desire to speak with someone who was gone from your life. Forever. Just gone.

"What about you?" she asked, voicing the question he'd been dreading.

He shrugged, too, saying, "They were spies for the U.S. government. Both of them died while helping a Communist defect to the United States."

And as he'd hoped, a smidgen of amusement shot through her eyes as she said, "Liar."

He laughed a bit, even though he'd never laughed

before when discussing his parents' deaths. "They were shot by the Mafia when a hit man mistook my father for a famous don."

She came forward and hit his arm then, saying, "Liar," on a huff of laughter.

And in a moment of total honesty, one that took him by surprise, he said, "They died in a car crash on their way back from a hunting trip. My mom and dad loved to hunt. It used to drive me nuts when they'd leave me behind. And then one day they were gone."

Her laughter faded, as did his smile, and they both felt a current of mutual understanding, one that said "I'm sorry." in a way that no words ever could.

"So," he said, once again trying to inject a lighter note. "Now that you feel sorry for me, and I feel sorry for you, we have to go to that dance tomorrow night, if only to drown our sorrows."

"They don't serve alcohol."

"For real?"

She nodded, her expression turning oddly pensive for a moment.

"Then we'll bring our own. We can have a tailgate party. Always wanted to have a tailgate party."

To which she just shook her head, her expression going back to impatient as she said, "I have a hard time knowing when you're serious and when you're not."

He took a step toward her, and this time the horse followed. Perverse creatures, horses.

"Where you're concerned, Amanda," he said, "I will always be serious."

And then he handed her the reins, saying, "Go put your horse away. *I'll* make us some breakfast."

...she'd done for reassurance, I'm only... No, she...
was sounding. If it wouldn't work, he'd...
her...p...see...and say, the time's over. Beringer.
pretty good wis...all the dirt, was...crossed him...
...it all.

Chapter Six

He was not, Amanda admitted as she readied herself
for the dance, what she'd expected. Not at all. Not
even a little bit.

She'd expected uptight and overzealous. But he
was fun and—all right, she would have to admit it—
a hard worker. Every task she'd given him today, and
yesterday, from doing his own laundry to mucking
out the chicken coop, he'd performed without com-
plaint. Most men she knew thought washing clothes
was women's work, but not Scott Beringer. He just
went about the job as if he didn't have a housemaid
who normally did the chore for him.

And here she was going on a date with him.

Okay, maybe "date" wasn't the right word. But
there was no denying that she primped for him that
evening. As she donned a denim skirt with appliquéd
running horses sewn around the hem, a silver concho
belt that hung loose around her hips and a black
stretch top that hugged her slender waist and accen-

tuated her breasts, she admitted to herself that she did so because of Scott. He may be Mr. Big City Man, but he was about to learn a country girl could look pretty good when all the dirt was washed off.

Of course, she should have figured her "date"—and she tried not to wince as she used the term again—would get his part wrong. It wasn't that he didn't dress western, he did. He just looked like a walking picnic table in his red-and-white-checkered shirt, which she recognized from their first meeting. It was obviously one of the few not destroyed by her bull. Pity.

"Wow," he said, and it was only then that she realized he was staring at her in a dazed kind of way. She watched as his eyes swept her up and down, and then those eyes of his narrowed—of course, the wolfish look he gave her was spoiled by the ten-gallon hat on his head.

"Yee-hah," he murmured.

And it was funny, because she'd have thought herself long past the state of needing a man's approval. Point of fact, she'd thought herself firmly in the I-don't-need-a-man phase. But as Scott eyed her up and down, she suddenly realized she wasn't as immune to the opposite sex as she thought. Specifically, *this* member of the opposite sex.

"You look great," he said.

"Thanks," she said. "You look—" She frowned, not wanting to insult him. "Good, too," she finished.

But she forgot that Scott was an intelligent man,

because he caught her hesitation, must have seen the way her eyes caught on his hat.

"What'd I do wrong?" he asked.

And it was so cute the way he asked. Like a kid who'd arrived home to find his parents at the front door waiting for him.

"Nothing," she lied.

"Is it the hat? Is it too big? I thought it looked kind of big in the store, but the saleswomen told me it looked great."

She almost lied again. Almost told him the hat was just fine. But she couldn't let him out in public looking like that. She'd once shown up at a school dance in a satin dress when everyone had been wearing jeans. The humiliation had been so extreme, her cheeks burned even now. It hadn't helped that she'd always been known as poor little Amanda Johnson, and that the dress had obviously been a re-tread of her mother's. Gosh. She could never consciously put someone in the same position.

"Let me put it this way…if you wear that thing on a plane, you won't need a parachute if it crashes."

He blinked at her, moved his lips as if he might smile, then said, "I was afraid of that."

"Maybe you should take it off," she said with an encouraging smile.

He did, the shirt he wore moving to reveal biceps that she'd noticed earlier were surprisingly sculpted. "Is that better?"

"You have hat head."

"Hat head?"

"Here," she said, coming forward. "Let me fix it."

She moved forward as she did so. She caught a whiff of him, the scent instantly reminding her of warm lips and a too hot tongue. Her body remembered, too, because suddenly she felt as charged as shag carpet. As she lifted her hand to his hair, a jolt went through her when she accidentally touched his scalp.

"Sorry," she murmured, because it hadn't been a figment of her imagination. She'd shocked him with a snap of static electricity.

"It's okay," he said. "I never knew your fingers could double as a cattle prod."

Their eyes met, and though Amanda had sworn off men, though she'd told herself after her last relationship that she would never, ever let sexual attraction sway her into a relationship with a man, she found that her hand had stilled, the limb suspended there as if held by a magnetic force. And that was the way her body felt, too: attracted. She leaned back, appalled to realize that she'd been staring at his lips.

"There," she said, though she hadn't done a thing. "That's better."

"I don't think so."

She looked up at him suddenly, surprised to see a feral look in his eyes. That masculinity was completely at odds with how she thought of him. He had an alpha maleness that directly contradicted his beta profession.

"You don't think what?" she found herself asking in a near whisper.

"That it's better."

"No?"

He bent down, lightly kissed her lips, and said, "Now, *that's* better."

It wasn't an aggressive kiss—well, it was a bit forward, but not in a bad way. This was a softer, gentler kiss than before, and yet every bit as neck-tingling as the first. And though the feral look didn't disappear, though she had the feeling he wanted to do more than peck her on the lips, he didn't. Instead he said, "How about the shirt?"

Shirt?

He held out his arms.

Oh, the shirt. "It's uh—" Man, what was *with* her? He was a computer geek. A Silicon Valley techie. Not the blue-collar type she was usually attracted to.

No, a voice said, she had it all wrong. He was one of the wealthiest men in the world. Powerful. Rich. Dynamic. And only at that moment did she understand why. People underestimated him. Beneath that little-boy exterior beat the heart of Tarzan. Tarzan with a slide rule, but Tarzan nonetheless.

"Should I change it?"

Change what? "Oh. Ah…" She stepped back. Didn't help. "Yeah," she said. "You need to wear something a little less…'' She thought a moment. ''Roy Rogers.''

''Roy Rogers?''

And gradually, every so slowly, she inserted the buffer, her mind warring with a healthy dose of sexual attraction.

''Yeah. You look like you should be leading Trigger.''

He released a huff of amusement. ''Thanks,'' he said.

''Do you have anything less checkered? And that isn't ruined?''

''I do.''

''Good. I'll wait here while you change into it.''

''Okay.''

But she didn't wait. The moment he disappeared, she was on the move, heading for her truck like an animal seeking refuge. And though she knew it was wrong, though she admitted what she was about to do was the equivalent of playing Ding Dong Ditch back when she was a kid, she left him. She was starting to like Scott Beringer entirely too much to trust herself on a date with him.

''YOU SHOULD JUMP HIS BONES.''

Amanda stared in mute horror and amusement as Flora, the more outspoken of the three ladies who comprised the ''Biddy Brigade''—as Amanda affectionately called the three older ladies who'd taken on the role of surrogate mother when her own mother had died—nodded her head.

"Seduce him," Flora said again. "That's what Alexis Carrington would do."

"Oh, you and that damn *Dynasty*," Edith said. "You watch entirely too much *Nick at Nite*."

"What the hell else am I supposed to do?" Flora— who also swore like a sailor—said to Edith. "There's not a man within fifty miles that's worth a lick of my time. And I mean that in its most literal sense."

"Flora!" Martha gasped.

"Prudes," Flora grumbled.

They were in the town hall, a single-story building that used to be a school back about a hundred years ago. Someone had laid down linoleum on the floor. Another person had made drapes out of a floral-print fabric. Around the perimeter walls were card tables with the auction items—homemade items like quilts and Flora's jam and pot holders with Home Sweet Home handwritten on them—a far cry, Amanda thought, from the usual items someone like Scott Beringer would be used to at his fancy-shmancy benefits.

The whole town had come tonight—kids varying in age from two to sixteen ran around the place while their parents socialized. Such was a Los Molina barn dance. They weren't in a barn, but people did dance at one end of the room. A string band comprised of two fiddles and a guitar shook things up with "Old MacDonald."

"It just doesn't seem fair," Edith said, shaking her

head. She wore her hair in a long braid down her back, just like she had when she was seventeen. Amanda knew this for a fact because she'd seen the pictures. At sixty-four she was still a looker, still rode horses—though the ranch she lived on had long since passed on to her son—and still competed on the seniors rodeo tour as a barrel racer. "Amanda's had enough tragedy in her life. And if that no-good man who calls himself her father had any kind of brain to speak of, he'd have never let this happen."

"I'm telling you, she needs to seduce him. Maybe not go all the way, but get him good and interested. Hell, maybe he'll get so hot and bothered he'll offer to pay her a million dollars just to have sex with him...like in that movie."

It was just like Flora to suggest such a thing. Just like Martha to protest, and just like Edith to complain. Nearing their seventies, the Biddies had been a part of Amanda's life since before she could remember. They'd changed her diapers, helped her get ready for her junior prom and held her together when Amanda's world had collapsed after her mother's death...and when she'd needed them.

And here they were for the next crisis in her life because Amanda had arrived at the barn dance utterly convinced that her days on the ranch were numbered. Scott Beringer not only seemed to enjoy working like a hired hand, he thrived at it. Not good. Not good at all.

And then there was that kiss.

Correction, those *two* kisses.

"That movie was a crock," Edith said. "Nobody in their right mind could believe Demi Moore would have relations with a man old enough to be her father. Not even for a million dollars."

"It's Dem-*me*," Flora said. "Dem-*me*. Say it right."

"I'll say it how I want."

"Children, children," Martha the mediator said. "Do we have to talk about this in public?"

"Why the hell not?" Flora asked.

"Because we shouldn't be talking about movies when our little Amanda has a problem."

To which both Edith and Flora said not a word, thank the good Lord, Amanda thought. Really, the last thing she needed was interference from the Biddy Brigade. As much as she loved them, sometimes they were a bit overwhelming.

"It just doesn't seem fair," Edith said again. "All those years of putting up with her father—" she looked at the other two Biddies as she continued "—and then Jake." She enunciated "Jake" as if it was a rare and communicable disease. "And now this. Amanda just got her life back on track, and that lump of coal she has for a father goes and messes it all up."

"Again," Flora added.

"Um, excuse me," Amanda said. "I'm still here. You don't need to talk about me as if I'm not in the room."

"I know that, dear," Martha said. "I just get so frustrated. I just wish I knew what to do."

"What is that?" Flora asked.

"I said I wish I knew what to do, not that I knew what to do."

"No, you big boobie. What is that noise?"

Leave it to Flora, who still had the ears of a cat, to notice the low rumbling in the distance.

"Is that your boyfriend, Edith? Did he fix that souped-up car of his again?"

"No," Edith said. "This sounds different."

"It sounds like a—" Martha squinted, as if it would help her to hear.

A helicopter, Amanda thought with a sudden stretch of her shocked spine. That sounded just like—

"A helicopter," Flora confirmed. "It's a helicopter."

And Amanda knew. She just knew, like she'd known before, that it was him.

The partygoers at the other end of the room slowly stopped dancing. Even the band quit playing one at a time. And outside, the sound of the helicopter got louder and louder.

"You think it's him?" Martha asked.

"Naah," Flora drawled sarcastically. "You think?" Then she looked at Amanda. "Guess you should have taken the keys to the chopper, too."

SCOTT WAS MAD. No other way to put it. After Amanda had ditched him he'd decided that what she needed was a reminder of just who, exactly, he was.

Billionaire.

Intelligent.

Geek.

So the last had slipped in there, but he couldn't deny that he felt a whole lot better about how he looked. He'd had his pilot pick him up, then fly him over to the western store that conveniently happened to be open late thanks to its location in an outlet center, one with an overlarge parking area where his chopper could land. After going straight to the manager and explaining the circumstances, he now found himself in the Wild West's version of corporate attire. A new pair of Wrangler jeans, a purple long-sleeved shirt with some kind of cowboy emblem on the front and a new black hat that the manager claimed would impress anyone who knew anything about hats. Scott didn't know a lick about hats, but this one had been expensive, and it was soft, and it fit low over his brow. Perfect for a man on a mission.

He pushed past the people who'd come out of the Los Molina Hall to see his helicopter land, and entered the building as if he owned it—which he could, if he wanted to.

It wasn't hard to find her. She was the only person in the fluorescent-lit room with her back turned to him, surrounded by three old ladies gawking as they caught their first glimpse of him. The room went completely quiet, well, more quiet than it had been before. It was an odd-looking room, with narrow windows spaced every five feet or so and a rectangular shape that made Scott think it might have been a school at one point, only now it'd been converted. He entered on the short end of the long rectangle, where Amanda stood in front of a dance floor. Those who had peered outside the windows instead of going outside stared at him as he entered, making Scott feel a bit like a gunslinger entering a bar.

Then he heard one of Amanda's companions say, "Hell, Amanda, if you don't do him, I will."

"Flora," one of the shorter, more compact ladies said. "He's young enough to be your son."

"Who cares?"

Scott almost smiled. Fact is, tonight he felt kind of handsome—a first for him, that's for sure. Of course, two gushing saleswomen—one of whom swore he looked like Clint Black—had helped to boost his self-esteem.

It was his newfound sense of self that made him strut a bit as he approached. No, not strut, swagger. He swaggered like a true cowboy, nodding to the ladies in Old West fashion as he came to a halt behind Amanda and said, "Woman, you've got some explaining to do."

He saw her shoulders stiffen, saw telltale signs that she recognized his voice. He thought she might ignore him. It seemed like something she might do, but she slowly turned. And *boy howdy* did he like the way her eyes widened, the way she parted her lips. The rest of her body stiffened as she caught sight of the new-and-improved Scott Beringer, but then she narrowed her eyes and crossed her arms. "So you made it?" she asked.

"Yeah," he said right back. "I made it, no thanks to you."

She shrugged. "I didn't think you wanted to go."

"Why in the heck would you think that?"

"Because I thought you felt obligated to go."

"Obligated?" he repeated in amazement, but then he told himself to calm down. He hadn't spent years reading body language not to know she was lying. And he didn't need a master's in psychology to know that she'd run away because she felt it, too, felt the snap and crackle that happened every time they were near. But it was more than that. It was the way everything had stilled around them for a brief moment after they'd kissed. The way they'd simply looked into each other's eyes. The way they'd both been slow to draw apart. Something was happening between them.

Scott was determined to find out what.

He glanced at the two women behind her, the three ladies looking between them with various degrees of curiosity and amusement on their faces. "Would you excuse us for a moment?"

"Sure," they said in unison.

"Hey," Amanda protested.

Scott held back a satisfied smirk.

"Oh, sure," she called. "Leave me. I'll remember

this.'' She hissed in frustration before crying out, ''Don't call me when you've fallen and can't get up.''

Which almost made Scott laugh, but he settled for goading her a bit by saying, ''Afraid to be alone with me?''

She turned back to him, and he had to admit, she was the best-looking woman he'd laid eyes on in a long, long time, especially tonight. Her hair hung wild down her back once again. She'd brushed something on her lashes that made her eyes look even more blue. That was the extent of her makeup. No blush, none of that paste women smeared on, just Amanda in all her organic glory.

''Of course I'm not afraid. Why would I be afraid?''

''Because you're attracted to me.''

''Because I'm what?'' she huffed, her hands going to her waist.

''Attracted to me,'' Scott said, and he wasn't sorry he said it. According to the dating book he'd read, this was called ''making the first move,'' and while he wasn't sure if putting his fate in the hands of *The Complete Idiot's Guide to Dating* would work, it was worth a shot. Hell, he needed all the help he could get.

Unfortunately, all ''making the first move'' seemed to do was make *her* spitting mad.

''Attracted to you? I am not attracted to you.''

''It's okay, you can admit it. I was a bit taken aback, too.''

"A bit—" She clenched her jaw. "Admit—"

People had started to file back in, he could tell because her eyes darted around. Behind him he heard one of the musicians pluck a fiddle string, a sure sign the music was about to start. He saw her try to gain control, and he had to admit, she was pretty good at it.

"Listen, you," she said in a near whisper, "I don't know what gives you the idea I'm attracted to you, but you're wrong."

"Then why'd you ditch me?"

"I told you—"

"Don't give me that 'you thought I felt obligated' nonsense. Be honest, Amanda. You left because you were afraid of the way kissing me made you feel."

"Why, you—" She pointed a finger at him, the same way she'd done the first day they'd met. "I did not ditch you out of fear. I ditched you because I figured if you really wanted to come to the dance, you'd find a way to attend, which you did." She crossed her arms in front of her again. "You're likely the first person in Los Molina history to arrive at the annual barn dance in a helicopter."

"Impressed?"

"No."

And that was what he liked about her. She really wasn't impressed. She was perturbed. And that was good, too. They were doing the "flirting flamenco," a least if he was reading her right, which he was. He hoped.

"Dance with me?"

The sudden change of subject made her blink. "What?"

"Dance with me."

"You're kidding, right?"

"No," he said.

"I don't dance at these things."

"Oh, sure you do."

They both turned to the woman who'd spoken, one of the ladies who'd been with her earlier, the one with a braid. "It's the one time each year that you get to kick up your heels. You told me so yourself."

Amanda looked over at her friend, her blue eyes narrowing in a way that said "Die, die, die," before she looked back at him again. "Ignore her," she said. "She has Alzheimer's."

"Do not," the woman said.

Amanda turned to her again. "Didn't he ask you for some privacy?"

"Sure, but I thought I better come over since you looked about ready to deck him."

"I was *not* going to deck him."

"Good." The woman turned toward him. "Edith Montgomery." She held out her hand. "Amanda tells me you've a real hard body. I see that she's right."

"Edith Montgomery," Amanda gasped in horror.

"Hey, if you're too frightened to go for it, I'm not."

Scott was having a hard time fighting his laughter. He held out a hand, saying, "Scott Beringer. And I'm flattered."

"You should be. I'm a hot commodity around here. Just ask the men at the Rosewood Community for Seniors. They all want in my pants."

"That does it," Amanda said. "I'm leaving." She turned to Scott. "Mr. Beringer, I hope you have a good time. Don't stay out too late because we have a long day ahead of us tomorrow."

"*You* can keep me from staying out too late."

"No, I can't. I think it only prudent to keep things on a professional level, Mr. Beringer. Edith, tell the other members of your coven good-night."

She turned on a heel and darted through the crowded building.

"Did she just call me a witch?"

Scott bit back another laugh. "I think so."

"Why, that little snot. I should have let her drown in her bathwater when she was an infant. Ungrateful brat."

To which Scott found himself smiling. He didn't know why, because the fact of the matter was, he'd just been rejected...again. Only it didn't bother him. Funny how that was. Instead it kind of made him feel, well, happy.

The three-piece band started up then, the square-dancing tune instantly making his left foot bounce in time to the music. He even bobbed his head a bit.

"Well, what are you waiting for?" Edith asked. "Go after her."

To which Scott looked at her, smiled even more, and said, "Thanks. I think I will."

Chapter Seven

Amanda should have fled from the building, but she just couldn't bring herself to run away from Scott Beringer. Ditch him, yes, but actually run? She had her pride.

But the minute she felt a hand on her arm, a breeze from the open double doors just ahead stirring fine hairs that clung to her face and made her nose twitch, she knew she should have obeyed her first instinct.

"Not so fast," she heard Scott say. "You still owe me a dance."

She turned on him, about to give him a piece of her mind, then she noticed all the covert glances they were getting. Not to mention the quickly approaching Stephanie Prichart.

"I don't owe you anything," she muttered in a low voice. "And I am not dancing with you, Scott Beringer."

"Please," he asked with a boyish yet endearing smile.

"No."

"Pretty please."

The man didn't know how to take "no" for an answer.

"Do you even know how to two-step?" she asked.

He stiffened, and his look of momentary chagrin made her gloat. "Ah-hah! I didn't think so."

"Teach me."

"Why?"

"Because ever since I was a little boy, I've wanted to swing to your pa'dner round and round. You're not going to disappoint me, are you?"

It amazed her the way he could make her forget he was a billionaire. And that he hadn't had the best childhood. And that she'd had dreams, too, as a kid, that had never been answered.

"One dance," she said.

He looked overjoyed, it all but melted her heart.

But as she led him to the dance floor she heard more than one person murmur his name as they passed. Word was out. Scott Beringer, recently voted America's "most eligible bachelor," a kazillionaire, and, yes, she could admit it, a good-looking guy, was in town. Terrific. By tomorrow she'd have every single woman in Los Molina at her doorstep.

She found the dance floor, scuffed from years of dancing feet—or more appropriately boots—which was placed at the end of the room. A platform about a foot off the ground held the three-piece band, all of whom were having a grand old time as they stomped their feet and swung their arms in rhythm to the beat.

"Do you know *anything* about two-stepping?" she asked, turning back to Scott as couples danced by them on the floor.

"I have two left feet, does that count?"

She resisted the urge to smile. "Unfortunately, no. Okay," she said, trying to be businesslike when, in fact, her heart had started to beat against her chest as if it wanted out. Now. "The rhythm is step-step-slow." She repeated it just in case he hadn't heard, dragging out the word *slow*. "Step-step, slo-o-ow," she emphasized again. "Like that," she added, indicating the couple who skirted the perimeter of the floor. It was Ben and Irene Perry, two people who'd been married for what seemed like an eternity, and who danced as if they'd been together as long, and who always made Amanda a little envious.

"Step-step, slow," Scott said, nodding. "I think I can do that."

He shouldn't look so cute as he concentrated on her words, she told herself. A man who'd stolen the family ranch, who insisted on kissing her at the oddest moments, and who all but melted her heart with his smiles, should not be thought of as cute. He should be thought of as…dangerous.

"Hold out your arms, like this." She demonstrated the man's position, her heart pounding in her chest in panic.

He did as asked, a grin appearing up the side of

his face as he held the stance for her approval. "I feel like a crossing guard without the stop sign."

Do not smile. Do *not* smile. "Now. I put my hands here." She placed said hands, one on his left shoulder, the other near the crook of his right arm, which bulged with a surprising amount of muscle. Dang. "When you feel pressure, move against it. You'll be going backward, which is harder, so it might not be easy."

"Oh, ye of little faith."

She lifted a brow. "Put your money where your mouth is, hotshot," she said, before pushing him backward and onto the dance floor.

She knew immediately that she'd been had.

He smiled.

She narrowed her eyes as he executed the steps perfectly, even took the lead and flipped her so *she* was going backward.

"Why, you—"

He laughed, his head tipping back as he navigated a corner of the wooden floor like a pro. She moved her hands to his chest, pushing against him in outrage, only to encounter a surprisingly buff chest, which she tried to ignore.

"Is your health insurance up to date, Mr. Beringer, because I have to tell you, I'd really like to trip you right now, and you might get injured."

He laughed again, grabbed her hands and pulled her toward him. "Come on," he said. "Let's kick up our heels."

She wanted to. She really wanted to. And that scared her even more.

"No," she said, pulling her hands out of his grasp and stopping. "If you know how to dance there's no need for a 'lesson.'"

"Watch out," he said, pulling her out of the way of a high-stepping couple.

She sidestepped, then looked up at him again, hands on her hips.

"Okay, okay," he said. "Quit with the laser eyes. I *knew* you'd say no to dancing with me, which is why I told you I didn't know how to dance."

"You were right."

"People are staring."

She stiffened, looked around her. People were, indeed, staring.

"Of course, if your object is to make a spectacle of yourself, by all means, keep fighting me. I am, however, not going to give up." He reached for her again.

She started to move away, but suddenly changed her mind. If she ran, he'd only follow. He'd already demonstrated that so instead she socked him with her eyes for a full five seconds—*whap, whap, whap*—before saying, "I should really tell you where you can stick it."

He smiled.

"Fine," she said, placing a hand on his arm, a part of her wanting to shake her head in exasperation, another part wishing she could come up with a good excuse not to dance with him. "Weasel," she added under her breath.

"Did you know weasels make good pets?"

She flicked her head to face him, some of her hair hitting him in the face. "Really? I heard they were nasty, disease-ridden vermin who kill more than they can eat."

"The ones in the wild are. But the ones that you tame actually make better pets than cats."

And what was that supposed to mean? She almost asked him, but she pushed against him instead. He stepped into the rhythm immediately.

"When'd you learn how to two-step?"

"Tonight."

"Tonight?"

"The gals at the store taught me. They also said if I do this—" He lifted his hand. "And this—" He twirled said hand. "You would—" She twirled beneath him. "Do that. Wow. Look. It works."

"You're a low-down, dirty snake."

"I know," he said, pulling her closer. "You should see me acquire companies."

SCOTT DIDN'T WANT THE DANCE to end. Frankly, when it did, he was going to try to keep her on the dance floor. But Fate took matters into her own hands—or feet as the case may be—because suddenly Amanda stumbled and cried "Ouch." Suddenly she winced in pain, then hopped up and down on one foot.

Scott narrowed his eyes, instantly suspicious. "What's wrong?"

"I think I twisted it," she said, hopping, hopping, hopping.

"Let me see."

"No," she said quickly.

Too quickly, Scott realized. Ah-hah, just as he thought.

"I need to get off the dance floor."

She was faking it. Scott would bet a percentage of his stocks on it. He thought about calling her bluff. Instead he decided to have a little fun. "Do you need to go to the hospital? I could have my pilot airlift you."

She stopped suddenly, her "injured" ankle held above the ground. *"What?"*

"Maybe it's broken."

"You would *airlift* me to a *hospital?*"

"Sure."

"Unbelievable," he thought he heard her murmur.

"In fact," he added for good measure, "I don't think you should walk on it. Let me carry you—"

"No," she said, lifting her hand. "I'm fine." She squeezed her eyes shut hard for a moment. "I mean, I'll be fine. Just let me sit down for a sec."

"I'll help you."

"No, no, no. I'm just going to go outside. You stay here."

He caught her as she was turning away, lifting her into his arms before she could tell him no.

"Scott Beringer," she cried, her thick hair cascading down around them, and from this view he could see she had a really narrow waist. And he could feel she had not an ounce of fat on her rib cage. "Put me down."

"No."

"Go get 'er, cowboy," a bystander said.

"Sweep her off her feet," said someone else—Edith, he thought.

He tried not to smile, even though Amanda wiggled in his arms like a freshly uncovered earthworm.

"You're going to make us fall," he said.

"Good, then I'll sue you for bodily injury, win a million dollars, and buy my ranch back."

"I hardly think a judge would believe I meant to harm you by carrying you in my arms because of your hypothetical injury. And it's your father's ranch, not yours."

"Hypothetical? What do you mean, hypothetical?"

They'd reached the entrance, the two doors still open wide. Some kids raced inside. Scott had to turn his body into a question mark to avoid hitting them. It was dark outside, and Scott couldn't help but look up in awe once they were outdoors. The sky was unbelievable. Not red from the glow of streetlights like it was in the Bay Area at night. Just dotted with so many brightly twinkling stars that reminded him of Amanda's eyes, eyes that were, well, he needed to be honest, *glaring* at him right now.

"C'mon, Amanda. Your ankle is no more injured than my ankle is."

"Why don't you let me kick you and we'll find out?"

"Temper, temper."

"Why shouldn't I be mad at you?" she asked as he gently set her down in the gravel parking lot, their feet cracking the rocks beneath. Cars were their only company, that and the crickets, the sound mixing with the music from inside. "You stole my father's ranch. And tonight you bullied me into dancing with you, and then I find out you lied about your dancing experience."

"I only did all that because I knew you wouldn't dance with me otherwise. And that I couldn't let happen."

"Why not?"

"Because, Amanda, I've wanted to hold you from the moment I saw you. Because you are, without a doubt, the most beautiful woman I've ever laid eyes on and I'm dying to kiss you again."

He felt her body tense, saw the way her eyes swept back and forth between his own as if wanting to avoid his gaze, but unable to do so.

"May I, Amanda?" he asked.

She didn't answer, and Scott didn't wait for one. He kissed her, not as Scott the nice guy. Not as Scott the geek, but as Scott the man. Funny thing was, instead of sparking off his lust, his first thought as he kissed her was that their lips seemed to fit together perfectly. That when he increased the pressure of his mouth, she seemed to know exactly what he wanted. That he didn't think he could have found a more perfect woman in the world to kiss.

She tilted her head, opened for him, their tongues touching each other's again. Then, *then,* the fireworks exploded. He pulled her even closer, stooped a little so his lower body was cradled in the valley between her thighs. And when he did, it was better than fireworks. Better, even, than he'd fantasized about while he'd been going about the chores she'd given him today.

And then they both pulled away at the same time, and it was only then that Scott realized it was because they'd both heard voices. He straightened. She pulled back a bit, too, but neither of them looked away. Scott knew it was because she was thinking the same thing as he.

She stepped back. And then stepped back again, wiping at her lips as if he'd left her with a bad taste, which, Scott thought, he was sure he hadn't. Breath mint. Five minutes ago.

"How do you do it?" she asked. "How do you make me forget that you've stolen my father's ranch? That you're only here because of some childhood fantasy you've had about being a cowboy?"

"I—"

"Mr. Beringer?"

They both stiffened. Turned.

"Mr. Beringer," said a boy who looked about ten,

but he might have been older or younger. It was hard to tell in the parking lot's half light. "My mom told me not to bug you, but I'm doing it, anyway, even though she said you and Amanda are arguing."

"Oh, great," Amanda muttered. "The whole town knows."

The boy looked up at her. "Hi, Amanda," he said.

"Hi, Sam," she mumbled back, shaking her head.

The kid looked back at Scott, his blond hair striking, as were his wide, blue eyes. "I was wondering," he began, his little Adam's apple bobbing as he swallowed. "See, I was wondering if I could ask you a question."

"Shoot, pa'dner."

The kid smiled at his Old West slang. "I was wondering if you ever have any old computers lying around." He swallowed again, looking back toward the hall, as if he expected his mother to come bearing down on them like Attila the Mother Hun. And maybe she would. "Computers that you, ah—"

"May not want?" Scott finished for him.

Sam nodded. "I have some money saved up," he said. "It's not much, but I could pay for a broken one, maybe, one I could fix. I love fixing things."

A kid after his own heart. "Nah," he said. And the crashing disappointment he saw on the boy's face made him add quickly, "You don't have to give me any money. I have lots and lots of computers."

The boy's face lit up. "Really?"

Scott nodded.

"Right *on*."

"But why do you want a computer so bad?" Scott couldn't resist asking, because if it was just so he could play video games—

"It's not for me. It's for my mom. See, she's going back to school and she's always having to stay late so she can use the computer lab at college. My dad left us a few years ago, so it's just her and me. But if she had her own computer, then she wouldn't have to stay late—"

Scott held up his hand. "Kid, you got yourself a computer. A new one, no less."

"Right *on*," Sam said again.

Scott smiled. He looked up at Amanda, surprised to see her shaking her head. When she caught his gaze, he could have sworn she had tears in her eyes. Then she turned on her heel and walked away.

Chapter Eight

The scene kept repeating in Amanda's mind the whole way home.

Scott Beringer was a nice guy...well, most of the time, anyway. And the way he'd handled Sam... The poor kid and his mom had had it pretty tough in recent years. Amanda's heart had gone out to them more than once. Having grown up with only one parent herself, well, if you could call a dad who'd been drunk half the time a parent. She knew what it was like to have to struggle to survive. To have to do what was needed to be done to better yourself. But for Scott to be so nice to a kid he didn't even know—

She shook her head, looking in her rearview mirror as if waiting to see Scott's helicopter behind her. She almost hoped he'd follow her.

Now, now, Amanda. Don't start softening toward the guy. Just because he's done one nice thing.

I'd buy you ten Thumpers.

Or two.

But he didn't follow. Then again, seeing as how he had a helicopter, he could fly like a crow, so to speak.

When she arrived home, the quiet of a spring evening was the only thing to greet her. Even though she cocked her head to listen for that *whump-whump-whump* off in the distance, she heard nothing but the sound of crickets and steers calling to one another in the distance. No helicopter in sight, though her headlights had caught a spot along the road where either a UFO had made a crop circle or Scott's pilot had picked a new landing sight. Either way, she suspected he was home, even though nothing stirred as she entered the front door.

She half expected him to jump out from a doorway.

But he didn't, so she made her way to her room, flipping on lights as she did so, but she was jumpy the whole way and kind of—all right, she could admit it—disappointed. First he hadn't stopped her from leaving. Then she'd kind of expected him to do a James Bond move with that helicopter. Only he didn't and she *was* disappointed, darn it because she'd realized tonight that she really shouldn't blame him for her dad's mistake, not when she had a feeling Scott would sell the place back to her if she really wanted it. The question was, did she? Was now the time to find that job breeding horses? Could she leave behind the only home she'd ever known in pursuit of that dream? She had once before. Did she have the courage to do it again?

She closed the door to her bedroom and leaned up

against it. So where the heck did that leave her? And if he would sell the place back, how the heck would she afford it? She had no idea, which only made her even *more* depressed.

She heard a creak.

Was it him?

Then she realized it was her own weight shifting that had caused the noise.

Darn it, she was losing her mind. She needed to get it together, she told herself as she changed into her flannel nightgown, skulked into the bathroom across the hall and brushed her teeth. When she opened the door a few minutes later there was still no sign of Scott, which only heightened her awareness even more.

He was doing this on purpose, she thought. She would stake her championship barrel-racing saddle on it, because as certain as she was of her determination to keep her distance from him, she had a feeling he had every intention of doing the exact opposite. And that made her feel—she closed her eyes as she lay in bed a little while later—turned on. No sense in denying it. She felt desired in the most basic of ways, and it made her feel more like a woman than she'd felt in, well, in a long, *long* time.

As she lay there, her body tingling and throbbing as she recalled their brief kiss, she tried not to panic too much at the thought of spending the next day with him…and the next…and the next.

She must have been more tired than she thought

because she fell asleep pretty quickly, waking with a suddenness that made her jerk up in bed. A glance at the clock revealed it was 8:00 a.m.—*8:00 a.m.!*

She'd overslept.

A held breath revealed it was quiet in the house. A glance out her bedroom window revealed that her dad had returned sometime during the night. That worried her, though it took her a moment to realize why. His boots were missing from the front porch, which meant he'd likely taken it into his head to do morning chores, something he shouldn't be doing considering the way his health was failing.

"Darn that man."

Quickly, she pulled on a pair of jeans so worn and faded they were three shades away from being white. Next she found and then discarded a T-shirt she'd had forever. Too many holes. Another one was too baggy, one was too tight—she almost grabbed that one, which made her wonder just who the heck she was trying to impress?

Scott? a little voice asked.

That made her angry all over again, so much so that she darted from her room, pulling her hair back into a ponytail as she did so, and telling herself that she didn't care if she ran into Scott on the way out. Of course, she didn't, but that didn't stop her from peeking around for him, so absorbed in her task she caught her elbow on the doorjamb as she met cold morning air.

"Ouch," she yelped, wiggling her tingling fingers. *Get it together, Amanda.*

Frowning, she took three steps at a time, heading toward the barn, figuring that was where her father would most likely be…and Scott.

"He's not here."

Amanda stiffened, turning toward her father, who was coming from the hay barn.

"Who's not here?" she asked innocently.

"Your boyfriend."

"He's not my boyfriend."

"Mmm-hmm," her dad said, and he lifted his brows at her just like he had the day she'd brought a saddle home she'd bought using credit.

"Um. Where is he?"

"Had to leave. Business, he said. Be back next week."

Next week?

She should be glad. Should be calling out "Whoopie." Only she was curiously, strangely…disappointed.

And from beneath the brim of his worn cowboy hat her dad said, "You better watch yourself, Amanda. That man is trouble, mark my words."

IT WAS ALMOST A WEEK to the day that Amanda pulled into the driveway and saw Scott riding in the arena. And it was strange how her heart leapt, though that was likely because her father had him on Rocket again. All week long she'd waited to hear from him, but he hadn't called. Not to say hi, boo, or otherwise. Her foot pressed down on the accelerator, and it wasn't until she was almost at the arena that she realized what she was doing. She stuffed her foot down on the brake.

He didn't even look up as she got out, just kept his gaze firmly fixed on Rocket, reins in hand, tan cowboy hat contrasting with his dark hair, though it matched his buff-colored denim shirt.

"Are you sure you want to do this?" her father asked as he walked toward…the back gate? What was he doing? "I only told you about this technique as a way of making conversation."

"I'm sure," Scott answered.

She closed the truck door just in time to watch Scott point Rocket toward the gate her father had opened, then push the cowboy hat more firmly on his head.

Uh-oh.

"Scott, no," she cried, but he didn't hear her. Or maybe he had but couldn't stop, because with a jab of his heels that would have done a rough-stock rider proud, Scott told Rocket to go.

The horse went, the gelding heading toward the open gate as if it was shot from a giant rubber band. Scott got thrust backward. His hand shot to the saddle horn. His hat flew off his head.

"The reins," she cried. "Pull back on the reins."

But the leather strips were too loose, and he was leaning too far back.

"Whoa," she ordered the horse, as if she was Dr. Dolittle and could talk to animals.

"Whoa doggie," her dad cried, his standard war cry when observing a good show.

"Whoa," Amanda tried again, running toward the arena. Ridiculous. As if she could sprout cheetah legs and catch Scott and a bolting horse. She gave up after a few yards and cupped her hands instead.

"Hold on, Scott," she yelled, and darned if he didn't, though how, she had no idea. Some root instinct long buried inside. He clutched the horse, leaned forward and rode off.

She turned on her dad as she stopped along the arena fence, dew making her hands wet as she set them on the white boards. "What in the heck do you think you're doing?"

Her dad, a man who'd chewed tobacco since before it came in cardboard cans, turned his head and spat on the ground, jerking his battered and worn straw hat low. "Teachin' him to ride."

"You'll kill him."

"Na-a-ah," he said. "He'll be fine. Best way for a man to learn how to ride is by doing it."

"Have you forgotten that you tried to teach my cousin John how to ride that way? And that he broke his collarbone as a result?"

Her father scrunched his face up, his hands hooking in his belt loops. "Guess I did."

"Ooh," Amanda huffed, turning away.

"You going after him?"

"Of course."

"Might want to bring that fancy cell-u-lar phone, just in case."

"Thanks, Dad. I appreciate the advice." Ooh, she mentally repeated as she headed for the house for said cell phone. Of all the fool, irresponsible things to do. Her dad had lost his mind.

And Scott, too. They should *both* be committed.

It took her less than five minutes to tack up Fancy in the cross-ties of the horse barn aisle, mostly because she decided to ride out bareback. Well, not entirely bareback. She strapped on one of the fuzzy pads she used when she was a kid—a bareback pad.

Fancy had been her horse for almost ten years. She seemed to know urgency was involved for she didn't take her customary five steps when Amanda swung up. Instead she stood stock still, her ears pricked toward the pasture, as if she could hear Scott's cries for help.

"Be careful," her dad said from behind her.

"It's not *my* health you need to worry about," she said as she kicked Fancy in the sides.

FINDING A LONE HORSE and rider in the midst of rolling acres was like searching for gold dust in a bathtub. It wasn't the size of the pasture. Amanda always laughed when people made a big deal about owning a hundred or two hundred acres. Fact was, two hundred acres was small for a cattle operation. What kept her from finding him was the dag-blasted hills. Tall, giant oaks, ones that were in full foliage this time of year, obstructed her view in some areas until she was so angry and so frustrated she vowed to put her dad in a retirement home.

In the end, it was more blind luck that allowed her to find him. She and Fancy crested yet another hill, one that overlooked a two-acre pond created for their stock. Relief caused her to just about slip from her horse when she spied Scott and Rocket at the shoreline, the horse's head lowered to the water as he drank deeply. Terrific. Next the horse would colic.

"Are you okay?" she called.

Why didn't you call? was her next question, though she kept it to herself.

Both Scott and the horse whirled, or rather, Rocket whirled and Scott stayed put. Odd how he seemed to hang in the air for a second before he splashed into the water.

SCOTT FELT HIMSELF FALL in slow motion. It was odd, because that was exactly what it felt like. He slid off one frame at a time, landing in the water back first.

"Scott," he heard Amanda say as his head broke the surface a few seconds later. "Are you all right?"

No. That water was *cold,* though thankfully not deep.

"Scott," she said again, sounding closer. A glance in her direction saw her all but galloping down the slope, panic on her face.

"I'm fine," he called. Man, he was tired of making

a fool of himself in front of her. He'd taken a week to pull himself together. Obviously, it hadn't worked.

"I'm sorry," she said. "I shouldn't have startled Rocket like that."

An apology. Progress.

"Head to the shore."

"C-c-can't," he said.

"Why not?"

"S-s-something's wrong with my legs."

She stared at him from shore, and darned if he didn't see her bite back a smile. He was positive of it because he saw her lower lip clamp down on her upper before she said with a stiff I'm-trying-not-to-laugh voice, "There's nothing wrong with your legs. They're just objecting to the ride you took."

He knew that. He wasn't an idiot. But, man oh man, if someone had told him it was possible to have one's legs hurt so much, he'd have never wanted to learn to ride.

"Get out of the water, Scott. You need to walk around a bit."

"H-h-hoping they'll g-go numb," he said. And he meant it.

"Look, if you stay out there you'll get hypothermia. That's spring water. It's cold. Besides, if you don't come out, you'll force me to rescue you. Again."

Again? When had she rescued him before?

Oh, yeah, the steer-feeding incident.

Fine. When she put it that way—

Taking a deep breath, something that was hard to do since his chest had contracted from the cold, he pushed off, his booted feet seeming to be held down by mud. Or maybe it was the cold. Or his sore muscles. He didn't know. One thing he did know, though: lower-extremity amputation was looking mighty good by the time he reached shore.

"Lord," he said, the cold morning air sticking to his wet legs like a block of ice. "My legs are wobbly."

"Here," she said, and in a motion that Scott envied—half feline grace, half athletic beauty—she slipped from her horse's back. He'd never be able to get off a horse like that. Not if he rode a month straight. But who was he trying to kid? He'd never be able to get back on a horse after today, not if his legs were any indication.

"Let me help you walk."

She came forward, slipping an arm around his waist. All thoughts of the kiss they shared last week must have fled from her mind because it was a purely impersonal touch. Not so, Scott. The minute she touched him, his legs warmed immediately, or rather, his groin did. And when she stared up at him from a face framed by wispy tendrils of her pretty red hair, her blue eyes concerned, he saw an opportunity.

Time to make his move. The one he'd dreamed of making the whole week he'd been gone, only he hadn't expected to be able to make it so soon.

"Ouch," he muttered, adding a groan for good

measure. If it'd worked for her last week, it could work for him, though he'd make sure she didn't know he was faking it.

She took the bait. "What's wrong?"

"I think my leg's rubbed raw." Well, that was true.

"Why don't you sit down?"

She helped to guide him to a nice comfy spot beneath an oak tree whose limbs were full of foliage. Grass sprouted up around them like a giant outdoor rug; dead winter leaves provided a cushion, too. Perfect. He clung to her, drawing her nearer. He could feel her right breast pressed against the crook of his arm. She wasn't wearing a bra. Even more perfect.

Yeah, and what are you going to do with bra-less breasts?

He didn't know yet, but he was sure going to find out.

So he contorted his face in pain and lay back. Above him a crescent moon glowed in the late morning sky, bright, as if it were still night. Birds called to one another. The horses had run off together, though they'd stopped to graze atop the embankment.

"Do you want me to rub your legs for you?"

He wanted her to rub something, all right.

One step at a time.

"Do you mind?" he asked.

And she did—rub them, that is.

And, dang, the feel of her touching him was as much a pain as it was a pleasure. It was as if his skin was ultrasensitized from the cold. As if her fingers were a heating pad that warmed him from the inside out.

"You're killing me."

She must have thought he meant her rubbing, because her strong fingers softened, became even more of a torture. He closed his eyes, moaned. She stopped. His eyes sprang open.

She stared at his manhood.

Uh-oh.

She jerked back.

Double uh-oh.

"What's wrong?" he asked innocently.

"What do you mean what's wrong?" she asked right back, staring *there* again. "You know what's wrong, you're…you're—"

"Hard?"

She looked away.

He sat up, trying not to groan as he did so. But when he reached to turn her head toward him, all thoughts of pain disappeared as he said tenderly, "I can't help it, Amanda. It's what you do to me. I've been gone a week and still all I can think about is how amazing you are and how much I want to kiss you."

Chapter Nine

Amanda felt the breath leave her.

How much I want to kiss you.

And the truth of the matter was, she *wanted* him to kiss her, too. Had thought about him doing exactly that the whole week he'd been gone. No sense in denying it. Now that she'd admitted he wasn't a jerk her interest in him had turned decidedly personal.

But…"I can't," she said, feeling disappointment and frustration.

"You can't what?"

"I can't get involved with you."

"Yes, you can."

"No, I can't. We're too different."

"I thought we were pretty good together."

"That's not what I mean."

"What *do* you mean?"

You disappear for a week.

But she refused to let him know how much that had bothered her.

"We should be getting back," she said instead. "You must be freezing cold."

"You like me," he persisted.

And she did. But that didn't mean she wasn't afraid to get involved with a man like him—so different from her. Heck, from a different world, one of computers and corporations while hers was animals and land. Not to mention he flew off to parts unknown at a moments notice. Once before she'd gotten involved with a man who'd thought of home as a place he changed his clothes. To say it hadn't worked out would be an understatement. That relationship had nearly destroyed her life. She'd become someone she didn't like, and a good friend had suffered the consequences. "I—Scott, please, don't press me. There's more to this than you know."

"Amanda, look, I may be a computer geek, but I'm also a man and I *know* you feel the same thing I do. Heck, it was all I could do not to come back sooner."

So he *had* thought of her.

So? What difference does that make?

A lot of difference.

She swallowed, her eyes following a concentric wave that rippled out from where a fish's tail had disturbed the surface near the shore.

"It won't work."

Scott moved, assuming the same position she did. He didn't touch her, and for that Amanda was grateful, and yet…she almost wished he would touch her.

That he'd somehow make her forget that he was Scott Beringer, computer genius and multi-kazzillionaire.

"Are you worried about the press? About living life in the public eye? Because if you are, there's no need. One thing I've noticed about fame, you're only as hot as that day's story. I've been a guest on TV shows where no one knows who I am until I introduce myself, and even then they don't care. I'm not a movie star or a professional ball player. I'm a computer geek who happens to have made a lot of money. Not very interesting."

She looked at him then, surprised to see that he actually believed that hooey. "Is that how you see yourself? As a computer geek?"

He shrugged. "Once a geek, always a geek."

"Why do you think you're a geek?"

He stared at her while waves gently lapped the shore, his eyes intense as he obviously debated with himself over something. "Justin Powell," he finally said.

"Who's Justin Powell?"

"Class bully. Seventh grade. Made my life hell. He said I probably 'did it' with my computers instead of girls. I was new to the school. Had just moved in with new foster parents. So I buried myself in binary code." He looked out over the water, too. "I was one of the few that used the computer lab and the other kids thought that was…strange."

Gosh, if only he knew how much she identified with him. It'd been no secret that the Johnsons were poor. Part of the reason why she'd thrown herself into getting a scholarship was so she could escape, maybe better herself. Maybe she still could.

"I tried to avoid Justin but he always seemed to know where I was."

"Did you tell your foster parents?"

He shrugged. And something about the look on his face, something about the way he wouldn't meet her eyes made her say, "You didn't have the best foster care, did you?"

He shrugged. "Some were good, some were bad, most were pretty indifferent."

She reached out and touched him. She couldn't stop herself from doing it. Compassion filled her. "How indifferent?" she probed.

He shrugged again, only this time he looked into her eyes. This time she saw a flash of pain and sorrow that made her own eyes instantly well with tears— she, the original cowgirl, a woman who prided herself on her toughness, had been reduced to tears twice since she'd met him.

"It was bad," she said, answering for him.

"Some were," he agreed, and it was funny because a moment ago she'd been all set to push him away. To tell him to back off. A moment ago she'd been close to laughter when she'd seen him fall off his horse. A moment ago she'd wanted him to kiss her. Now *she* wanted to kiss *him*.

"But you survived."

"I survived," he echoed.

"In spite of it all."

He looked at her then, and at that moment something changed, something that made her still. He stared down at her and then his head dropped, moving closer...closer still.

Move! her mind screamed.

But she didn't. Unbelievable. Totally unbelievable how perfectly their lips fit together. It was as if they were born to kiss each other. As if they'd been put on Earth just for that purpose. And then her body jump-started like an old motor. It didn't matter that he was wet, and that as she lay back, she drew Scott with her. That her own legs soaked up that wetness. That the grass felt equally damp and that old leaves pricked her scalp. All that mattered was the way Scott's tongue felt as it brushed against hers, the way he moaned, they way he felt against her hands. Sculpted. Hard. Man.

How, she distantly wondered, how did he do it? How did he look like such a desk jockey yet have the muscles of a marathon runner? Hard, sinewy cords ran down his arms, harder up near the shoulders, yet just as firm across his chest. She pulled her lips away, pressed her palms against the ridges of that chest, stared into smoky eyes as he drew back to look at her, too. Their gazes held as she undid a button on his buff-colored denim shirt, and then another and another until she'd exposed not the pale flesh of an office worker, but the tanned, taut muscles of a man. A sexy, hard body of a man.

"You're not what I expected," she said.

"Funny," he answered, his eyes never leaving her own. "You're what I've always wanted."

Her breath caught.

And then he was kissing her again, and that was good, because she suddenly couldn't breathe, suddenly felt tears come to her eyes again, because the tenderness in his eyes as he'd said those words was as unmistakable as the look of desire that followed the words. And then his hand slipped to the waist of her jeans, his fingers tugging at her own shirt until his hand could explore her own flesh, flesh that jumped at his touch, only to do more than jump when his lips replaced his hand. She arched her back because her whole body seemed to tighten and then pulse at the feel of his teeth suddenly nipping at the juncture of her legs.

Dying. She was dying. She dug her hands into the grass.

"Scott," she moaned.

It had to be the fact that she hadn't had sex in months. Years. How else to explain this wild and wicked urge to part her legs? To give this man, this virtual stranger, access to her most private parts?

Then he moved and slipped a hand between her legs, and she almost came off the ground.

Too fast. Too hot. Too heavy and, yes, darn it, she wanted him. She couldn't explain why. At this point, she didn't care. She let him stroke her. Let him part her further. And when he moved again, she let him kiss her. Let him kiss her in a way that made her feel more like a woman than she'd ever felt before. Sexy. Desired. *Wanted.*

Jake had made her feel tolerated. Never, *ever* had Jake made her feel like a woman.

Scott went right on kissing her. Right on tormenting her with a rhythm between her legs and in her mouth that lifted her closer and closer to a climax.

He pulled his lips away again, turned his head so that they were cheek to cheek. "That's it," she heard him moan. "That's it. Let it happen. Let it go."

That he knew enough about her already to tell when she neared her peak amazed her. That he didn't strip down himself and take what she would have given him impressed her. That he whispered naughty words to her that she'd only ever heard in her fantasies was her undoing.

She arched her back, felt the pulse begin to build, felt her body tighten and then release with a sweetness that brought tears to her eyes.

And all he did was hold her. He didn't do anything else but that. As she drifted back to reality, a part of Amanda waited for him to move, to get undressed so he could enjoy his own release. When he didn't, she opened her eyes, drew back to look at him.

What she saw took her breath away. Tenderness. And pride. And amusement. The pride was obviously for himself and his ability to bring her to climax.

She understood the amusement a second later when he said, "Our horses have run away."

AND THAT WAS IT. That was all he said, just helped her up, even though she could see the bulge in his jeans. She almost asked him about that bulge. Almost asked him if there was something she could do to help alleviate his, er, pain.

He must have read her mind because he met her eyes and said, "Don't worry. I'm more concerned that you enjoyed yourself."

More concerned about *her?* Had she heard him right?

Apparently so because he turned away from her then and said, "I guess we're walking."

"I guess we are," she said absently because, darn it, she didn't know what else to say. She couldn't believe she'd let him do…do, well, *that.*

"There you are."

They both looked up, both froze. Her father and his horse stood silhouetted by the late morning light, a dark shadow against a blue backdrop.

"I found these two a few hills over," he said, motioning with his head toward the two horses he led—one on either side—his voice running downhill with ease. "You two okay?"

"Hi, Dad," she said, her cheeks heating like a forge when she realized her shirt still hung out of her jeans, and that Scott was in the process of buttoning up his shirt.

Dang. Dang, dang, dang. She'd never hear the end of this.

She heard a cluck, saw her dad's big palomino horse take a step toward them. Gingerly, the quarter horse made his way down the slope, and as her father rode toward them, the sun blocked by the hill he rode down, she saw his eyes going between the two of them, back and forth, back and forth. Amanda felt like a kid who'd been caught sneaking in late from the prom.

"Honey," he said with a look she remembered from her youth. "Take your horse. I want to talk to Mr. Billionaire alone."

"Daddy."

"Go," he said without ever, *ever* looking her way. She went.

THIS MUST BE WHAT A cattle rustler felt like when he stared into the eyes of a local sheriff, Scott thought as Amanda's father stared down at him. He looked the part of local law, too, right down to his beige cowboy hat and thick denim jacket. The horse he rode pinned his ears, almost as if he felt his master's disapproval. Scott reminded himself that he'd recently been chewed out by the president of the United States for "lack of party support" as he called it. Scott could handle Amanda's father.

Right?

Right?

But as her father leaned over the side of his horse, tipped his hat back with a gloved hand, then put his face about a foot from Scott's, the boy wonder of the computer industry suddenly felt about four years old.

"Is she gone?" he asked.

Scott looked past Mr. Johnson's horse's white mane to Amanda, who was leading their own mounts away. "Yeah."

Mr. Johnson straightened again, and it was the weirdest thing because the expression on his face changed right then. It went from mean as a snake's to, to…well, to wily as a coyote's.

What the—

"Can she see us?" he asked next.

Scott looked over at Amanda again. "No."

"Good," he said. "Look, you're doing okay, but you need to move fast. Amanda's likely to balk if she thinks too much about something. Like her mother in that way. Used to drive me nuts. 'Course, it's one of the things I miss most about my wife, but you don't need to hear about that. Just hurry things up a bit. Sweep her off her feet. Take her for a ride in that fancy whirlybird of yours. Just do it quickly. And no more disappearing for a week."

Scott blinked. Not sure he'd heard right.

"What?"

"And don't let on that I approve," he added. "If Amanda thinks I like you she'll balk like an unbroken filly. It'd be just like her to take it into her head not to get involved with you just because I want the two of you to get involved."

"You want me to date her?"

"'Course I do."

"But— What about the ranch?"

He waved a hand, then rested it on the rubber-wrapped saddle horn. "It was me who didn't pay the taxes. I knew what was coming down. Amanda got her knickers in a twist because I didn't tell her, but my problems are my own, and fact is, I didn't realize until too late how much the place meant to her. And that's twice now I've done something like that to her. Figure she's probably had it about up to here with me." He brought his gloved hand up to his forehead. "But the fact is I'm sick. Amanda knows it and I know it. I'm worried about her. This place is too much for her to manage on her own. But now that you own the place..." He let his words dribble off.

"You're matchmaking," Scott said.

Roy emitted a snort that sounded like one of his bulls. "Playing the odds," he corrected. "Look, it may not work out between you, but at least she's showing some interest. I haven't seen her so worked up over a man in, well, a long time. You should'a seen her the week you were gone. 'Bout tore my head off. But you better hurry. Amanda hasn't had the best of luck with men. If she thinks too much on this, you'll spook her. I'll keep doing my part to get you two together, but you need to do your part, too."

Scott stiffened, having to suddenly realign his whole way of thinking about Roy Johnson. "Why do I have the feeling that sending me off on Rocket this morning was no accident?"

"It wasn't. Knew she'd go after you, even if it

meant I had to call her on that fancy cell-u-lar phone of hers to come home and help me find you."

Unbelievable. He'd been manipulated.

The old cowboy straightened on his horse again, and his expression went back to mean as a snake as he pulled his hat low on his age-spotted forehead, bits of gray hair sticking out. But then he leaned toward him again. "That said, if you break her heart, I'll break your neck." They stared into each other's eyes. "Understood?"

"Understood." Scott swallowed, adding a "sir" at the end.

To which Amanda's father nodded, his lips pressing together again as he leaned back and said, "Hop to it, son. You don't have much time."

And with that the man clucked to his horse, pulled on the reins and pointed the palomino toward Amanda. Scott could only blink.

Chapter Ten

It was the longest ride of Amanda's life. Long and humiliating because her dad kept shooting them both disapproving looks. Amanda hadn't felt so mortified since the time Roy had caught her smoking in the bathroom. Still, it surprised her a bit that her father seemed to disapprove. Granted, Scott had stolen the family ranch, but she'd never seen her father so downright rank. He kept shooting Scott snake-venom looks, tugging his hat low over his brow as if he were about to mow Scott down with a six-shooter.

When they got back to the ranch, all Amanda wanted to do was retreat inside the house.

"Put the horses up," she ordered Scott, and when he looked a bit miffed at her autocratic tone, she added, "I have some things to do inside." Which they both knew was a bunch of hooey, not that Amanda cared. Nor did she care that Scott looked a bit pained when he dismounted.

"I swear I can't feel my legs," he said.

"Move around. You'll feel better."

"I'd rather lie down in a bed."

She nodded.

"With you," he added, which made Amanda blush like a girl on her first date.

"Sorry. Can't help you there."

"That's not the impression I got earlier."

Which was something she didn't want to be reminded of. In fact, what she wanted to do was slink away somewhere and think about exactly that. Or rather not think about it. Or maybe think about it and then figure out what the heck it all meant. Or didn't mean. Or—

Stop it! she ordered herself. "I'll be inside if you need me," she said, turning away.

"Oh, I need you, all right."

But Amanda ignored him, even as her cheeks turned as red as a Radio Flyer wagon. Terrific. Just what she needed. Scott making flirtatious remarks, remarks that, darn it all, made her feel all hot and bothered.

She had mad cow disease. Because she sure as heck must be losing her mind if she was contemplating a relationship with Scott Beringer.

Relationship. Hah. More like fling. One-night stand. Sex. Because she sure as heck wasn't stupid enough to believe he'd be sticking around the farm for her, despite his silly idea to become a cowboy.

Slamming the front door behind her, she stomped into the kitchen. Her message light blinked, and for a moment the hope that it was the bank calling her back about the loan she'd applied for filled her with anticipation. She stabbed at the play button with enough force to bend her nail back.

"Amanda." Stephanie Prichart's voice filled the room as Amanda shook her hand in pain. "It's me, Stephanie. Hey, I was wondering if Scott might be interested in riding in the celebrity team-roping event at this year's rodeo. I know it's kinda short notice, but you're such a whiz with teaching people how to ride, I bet you could get him to throw a rope in a heartbeat. Would you mind asking him if he'd like to do it? I already called Chase and he has a horse he can use. And if he rides, I'll bet we'll get tons more press coverage, which means more money for the shelter if ticket sales increase, and, well, it'd be just great. If you could ask him, I'd really appreciate it. Thanks. Bye."

When the beep sounded the end of the message, Amanda stared at the machine as if it'd started singing the national anthem.

Teach Scott Beringer how to rope?

In four weeks' time?

Stephanie must have eaten a mad cow.

"Sounds like fun."

Amanda just about jumped out of her underwear. "What the—" She turned toward the kitchen door. "There is no way you're done putting those horses up."

Scott shuffled into the kitchen, shuffled because she

could tell he was still hurting after his ride. He'd found his straw hat—although she suspected it was really one of those palm hats—out in the arena, too, the thing pulled low over his brow. Like her dad's.

"Relax," he said. "Your dad offered to take care of the horses."

"And you let him? He shouldn't be riding, much less cooling horses out."

"Amanda," Scott said, grabbing her arm as she made to move past him. "Your father's capable of doing a lot more than you think. Let him. He enjoys it."

"Enjoying it isn't the point," she said, moving away from him because, darn it, when she felt his fingers on her arm all she could think about was those same fingers…

Doing…

That.

She warmed between her legs.

"What's he sick with, anyway?" Scott asked, and she was surprised to see the note of genuine concern in his voice, especially given the glares her father had given him all the way home.

"Diabetes," she said. "He's had it for years, not that you'd know it looking at what he eats and drinks. Unfortunately, it's caught up to him now."

"Is it his kidneys?"

"That and other things. It's why I came home after college. He needs help." She tried to move past him again.

"Amanda, let him be. Exercise is good for him. I know. My mom was a diabetic."

She didn't think it was possible for him to surprise her, but every time Scott revealed another facet of his past, it generally did.

"She managed her disease with diet and exercise," he said. "I'm sure your father can, too. If you'll let him."

"It's too late for that, Scott. I wish it wasn't, but it is."

"Then let him pretend for a moment that he's not sick. If he needs help, I'm sure he'll ask for it."

"You don't know my dad," she muttered under her breath.

"No, but if he's anything like you, I'm sure he'll surprise us both by living to a ripe old age."

Had she been complimented?

"Let him take care of the horses, Amanda. He told me they just needed to be unsaddled. Surely he can do that?"

He could. She knew he could. She needed to—

Escape.

That was what she really wanted.

"Now," Scott said. "What is this team-roping thing and when can you start teaching me to do it?"

"Do it? Are you nuts?" And Amanda momentarily forgot about their time at the lake and her father's failing health and the need to escape. "You can't possibly learn how to rope a steer in four weeks' time."

"I can try."

"Without me."

He shook his head, crossing his arms in front of her. "And here I thought you were the type of person who'd want to help raise money for a homeless shelter."

"Oh, that's low. That's really low. And it's a children's shelter."

"Even more of a reason to teach me how to rope."

"Impossible."

"You forget who you're dealing with."

But that was the thing. She did know whom she was dealing with. The man constantly threw her off guard. He was like a Cracker Jack box that revealed a really cool and unexpected prize inside. "You think just because you've got a genius IQ you can learn to rope a steer in record time?"

"I bet I could."

"Your arrogance is amazing."

"I thought what we did earlier was pretty amazing."

"Please don't bring that up."

"But we should, Amanda. We should talk about what happened. And where we're going with this."

"We're not going anywhere." She turned on her heel, determined to leave him in the kitchen this time if it meant using a cattle prod to keep him away.

"I'll take that bet, Amanda."

She told herself to ignore him, even as she waited for him to follow her outside, which he did, his new boots *clomp-clomp-clomping* on the wooden deck.

"I bet I can learn to rope a steer faster than you cried out my name by that lake."

It's a stock pond, she almost snapped in exasperation.

"In fact, I'll make you a deal," he called out from the top of the porch. "I'll sell the ranch back to you for a dollar if I can't rope a steer in less than—how long did it take for me to pleasure you? Two minutes? One?"

The words brought her up short. And even though she turned around only to note that he looked as handsome as a model on a Wrangler poster as he leaned against a post, she was proud of the way she managed to contain her instant pique as she said, *"Pleasure me?"*

He took the steps slowly as he said, "Yup."

"You've got a lot of nerve, buddy."

"Well?" he asked. "Will you do it?"

"Do what?"

"Accept my bet?"

"You're kidding, right?"

He shook his head.

"You think you can rope a steer in less than *ten* minutes?" she asked.

"Ten? It wasn't ten."

"Yes. It. Was."

He lifted his hands. Big hands, they were, and looking more work-worn than when she'd first met him. She liked that.

"Fine," he said. "Ten minutes."

And for a moment she had to work to remember what it was they were talking about. Oh, yeah, he was betting her—

"I bet I can rope a steer in less than *ten* minutes." And it was really strange, because she could have sworn she saw a crafty look of glee enter his eyes just before he said, "Of course, now we have to decide what you'll give me if I win."

She felt like her brain was a carton of eggs that had just been dropped on the ground. Hard. "What do you mean?"

"What's your favorite restaurant?"

"Why?"

"Just tell me."

But she had a feeling she knew where this was going so she said, "Burger Barn."

"C'mon. What is it?"

"What does it matter?"

"Because if I win I want to take you on a date. A *real* date. On my turf. Nice dress. Fancy restaurant. My treat."

"Do you really?"

"Really," he answered.

A date. But then she stiffened as a fragment of what he'd said earlier came back.

He'd sell the ranch back to her.

"Did you really mean it about selling the ranch back to me?"

"Yup. If I lose."

"You're on," she said.

The Harlequin Reader Service® — Here's how it works:

If offer card is missing write to: Harlequin Reader Service, 3010 Walden Ave., P.O. Box 1867, Buffalo NY 14240-1867

NO POSTAGE
NECESSARY
IF MAILED
IN THE
UNITED STATES

BUSINESS REPLY MAIL
FIRST-CLASS MAIL   PERMIT NO. 717-003   BUFFALO, NY

POSTAGE WILL BE PAID BY ADDRESSEE

HARLEQUIN READER SERVICE
3010 WALDEN AVE
PO BOX 1867
BUFFALO NY 14240-9952

Play the Lucky Hearts Game

and get...
2 FREE BOOKS
and a FREE MYSTERY GIFT...
YOURS to KEEP!

yes! I have scratched off the silver card. Please send me my *2 FREE BOOKS* and *FREE mystery GIFT*. I understand that I am under no obligation to purchase any books as explained on the back of this card.

Scratch Here!
then look below to see what your cards get you... 2 Free Books & a Free Mystery Gift!

▲ DETACH AND MAIL CARD TODAY! ▲

354 HDL DU6Y   154 HDL DU7G

FIRST NAME	LAST NAME

ADDRESS

APT.#   CITY

STATE/PROV.   ZIP/POSTAL CODE   (H-AR-09/03)

Twenty-one gets you
2 FREE BOOKS
and a **FREE MYSTERY GIFT!**

Twenty gets you
2 FREE BOOKS!

Nineteen gets you
1 FREE BOOK!

TRY AGAIN!

It was the perfect solution. If he lost the bet, he'd have to sell. She wouldn't have to ask him, or beg him, or do something underhanded to make him hate ranching life.

"Great," he said. "When can that guy Chase bring over that horse?"

"I'll call and find out."

"Good. I'll just wait here."

And he looked so utterly self-confident, so completely unlike that beta male she'd pegged him for, for a moment Amanda wondered if she'd been had. But, no. The bet was as good as won. No need to worry. No need at all.

THREE HOURS LATER, hours during which Amanda avoided him as if he were a walking cow patty, Scott watched as a brown horse was backed out of a fancy horse trailer that was the equivalent of a horsey RV.

"You have AC in there?" Scott asked the broadshouldered man who held the horse's lead rope.

He shook his head, a black hat low over his brow. "Just in the living quarters."

Scott nodded. "You must travel with your horses a lot."

"Chase Cavanaugh is a stock contractor," Stephanie Prichart said with a note of pride in her voice. "And a six-time all-round world-champion cowboy."

"Wow," Scott said, impressed, even if he didn't know what a "stock contractor" was. "I guess that means you must be pretty good."

The man shrugged, tying his horse to a ring welded into the side of the trailer. When he was finished, he turned to Stephanie and ignored him. "Where's Amanda?"

"She's inside," Stephanie answered.

"And Roy?"

"He said he'd be out in a minute."

The man nodded.

"Chase," Stephanie said. "I'm really grateful to you for bringing Houdini over on such notice. I know you're busy this time of year."

"You caught me between rodeos," he said. "So it's not a big deal. Tell Amanda he's an easy keeper. Likes to untie himself, so she'll need to pull the rope through the slip knot to keep him from escaping. Why I call him Houdini."

"Are you going to stick around?" Stephanie asked.

The man called Chase looked at Scott then, and it was kind of funny because up until that moment Scott hadn't thought of the man in terms of competition, but suddenly, he did.

"Wouldn't miss this for the world," he said.

The sound of gravel crackling under four wheels caught Scott's attention. A silver Honda headed toward them, a man behind the wheel.

"That must be Tim from the paper."

"Paper?" Scott asked.

"Yeah," Stephanie said, turning to face him. "I thought we could generate some advance interest in the rodeo if they did a story on your determination to learn how to rope."

"Great," Chase grumbled as he came from the back of the trailer with a saddle in hand, the thing hanging on his hipbone the way Scott'd seen in cigarette ads. "They can take pictures of him breaking his neck." He shifted his hands, swinging the saddle up, not even sparing Scott a glance as he settled the thing on his horse's back.

"For your information, I've ridden every day since coming here."

"Yeah? And how many days is that?"

Scott felt just like he used to feel when confronted by the class jock. "Three, but I'm a fast learner."

"Doesn't take much learnin' to fall off," Chase mumbled.

"Is that why you became a rodeo rider?" Scott asked. "Because it's easy?"

Chase paused in the middle of what Scott now knew was called "girthing up." He gave Scott a look, one that seemed almost amused. "Actually, yeah," he said, before pulling up on the leather with a grimace and causing the horse to grunt.

Scott almost said something else, but Stephanie interrupted him with "Here comes Amanda."

Scott turned, and—man—did she look good. It amazed him the way her hair swirled around her— she looked like one of those women in a shampoo commercial. And then his eyes narrowed as he wondered just why it was that her hair was brushed till it shone. Why she wore a clingy light green T-shirt that read Cowboy Up across her breasts. Which Cowboy Up? he wanted to know.

Scott turned his head, looked at Mr. Six-Time All-Round World-Champion Cowboy, the man staring at Amanda as if she were the oats in his bucket.

"Hey, Amanda," he said.

"Hey, Chase," she answered softly.

"I see you've taken on a new project," Mr. Cowboy said.

Scott waited for her to defend him, to explain that he was far more to her than a "project," but she just smiled and said, "I had nothing to do with this. My dad's up to his usual tricks."

"Mr. Beringer?" a young man's voice said from behind him. "Wow. It really is you. I'm Tim from the *San Jose Mercury*."

Scott almost ignored the voice, his gaze flicking between Mr. Rodeo Dude and Amanda. And then Chase looked up at him and smirked.

That did it.

Scott had never liked jocks. Justin Powell, his high school nemesis, had pounded that into his head. Literally.

A face obstructed his view. "Hi," Tim from the *Mercury* said.

Scott tightened his lips and pulled his gaze away from Mr. Dropped on His Head One Too Many Times.

"Hi, Tim. Nice to meet you," Scott said, holding

out his hand. The kid looked like a lollipop with an overlarge head and rail-thin body. Young with acne-scarred skin, black hair and wide brown eyes, Tim had Scott almost feeling sorry for him. Might have, too, if he wasn't so incensed with Amanda's friend.

Tim looked a little awestruck, which made Scott feel a bit better until he saw Amanda smile at Chase before turning to get Houdini's bridle from the rear closet—or tack room—or whatever it was called.

"Did Stephanie tell you about the bet?" Scott asked Tim, who shook his head no before hurriedly grabbing pen and paper. Scott pressed his lips together. But why not? Why not give the kid a story? In a low voice so Amanda couldn't overhear—not that she was likely to, what with her and Chase all cozylike—Scott filled the reporter in.

"So you have ten minutes to rope a steer?" Tim asked.

"Yeah, but it won't take me that long."

"It won't?"

This time it was Scott who shook his head, drawing a smirk on his own lips. "Nope."

"And what do you get if you win?"

This was the best part. "A date," Scott said.

Tim's eyes widened. "For real?"

"For real," Scott said, giving him a full-fledged smile now.

"With who?"

"Amanda Johnson."

"Cool. Our readers will love this. Billionaire Bets for a Babe."

"A babe?" Yeah, she is that.

"Ready?" Chase asked, turning Houdini toward Scott just as Roy Johnson joined them, his only indication that he wished Scott good luck was a wink that he didn't let the others see.

Scott straightened, looking at Amanda as he said, "I'm ready."

"Let me go load the steers," Amanda said, turning away from him.

Scott looked at Chase. "I just have to go get something from the barn. I'll be right back."

Chase didn't seem to care if he had to travel to the moon. He shrugged, then turned his horse toward the arena.

"What are you getting from the barn?" Tim, the intrepid reporter, asked.

"Why don't you come with me and I'll show you."

Chapter Eleven

He held a fishing pole in his hands when he came back from the barn. Amanda couldn't believe her eyes.

"Actually," Scott said to her when she asked him what he was doing with a fishing pole, "this is my soon-to-be-patented Acme steer-catching pole."

Steer-catching *what?* Amanda stiffened.

"Somehow, I don't think the Professional Rodeo Cowboy Association would approve," Chase said in a monotone.

Amanda almost turned toward her longtime friend, but she just couldn't take her eyes off the thing in Scott's hands. It was a PVC pipe, about fifteen feet long or so, with a noose hanging out of one end. The other end of the rope trailed from the opposite hole, the thing resembling a fishnet, without the net.

"You can't be serious."

"Sure I am," he said. "You never specified how I was to catch the steer, just that I was to catch it."

"Why you— That's cheating."

"Technically," the reporter said, "it's not, as I'm sure our readers will agree."

"Your readers?"

"He's from the *Merc,*" Scott said smugly. "He's going to write about how I won my bet and got a date with you."

"He's *what?*" Amanda cried.

"Going to—"

"No, no, no," she interrupted. "No one's doing a story on this."

"Actually, Ms. Johnson, I am," said the reporter. "It's called freedom of speech."

It's called freedom of speech, Amanda silently mimicked. Whelp. She ought to boot him from their land. Except it wasn't her land, which made her feel…resigned. Outsmarted. Again. "You'll never get near Houdini with that thing," she pointed out.

Which turned out to be totally untrue, because Houdini was the type of quarter horse that nothing seemed to bother, including fifteen-foot-long pieces of white pipe with a lasso hanging off the end of it.

"Unbelievable," Amanda said as Scott was handed the pole. He looked like a knight of old with a very odd looking lance. Oddly, it made her want to laugh.

"He used to be a drill-team horse," Chase explained. "Probably thinks it's a flag."

And the horse probably did, but that didn't mean Scott's "invention" would work. Please, Lord, don't let it, Amanda thought. She didn't want to beg him to sell the ranch back to her. Or go on a date with him, either.

Amanda gnashed her teeth together, actually ground the enamel together so that it creaked in a satisfying way, which was about the only satisfaction she'd get, if she didn't miss her guess.

"I can't believe this," she found herself muttering.

And all Scott did was smile.

"Actually, it's a pretty ingenious idea," Roy Johnson said as he moved closer.

Amanda whirled on her father. "Dad. I can't believe you. He's *cheating.*" ·

"No, he's winning a bet. Gotta respect that."

Amanda stared at the faces surrounding her, each of which stared back at her with various degrees of amusement, sympathy and even—in Stephanie's case—glee. And it was then she realized she fought a losing battle.

"I'll work the chute," Stephanie said as Scott sorted the reins, the pole and himself atop the horse. He grimaced inspite of the painkillers he'd wolfed down earlier.

"Ready?" Stephanie asked as she put her hand on the release mechanism.

"Ready," Scott said with a look on his face that would have done a professional team roper proud, except his Acme steer-catcher spoiled the whole image.

Amanda glumly crossed her arms in front of her as

she watched Scott settle the horse into the header box.

"You gonna need me to haze?" Chase asked her.

"Why make it easier for him?" Amanda muttered knowing she'd lost her chance at the ranch. Darn it.

Scott took his position, her dad—of all people—moving a steer into the chute. Scott had obviously seen it done on TV because he positioned Houdini exactly right, either that or someone had educated him. He took a tighter grip on the pole as he nodded for the steer to be released.

Amanda hoped it wouldn't work, or the very least she'd hoped it would take eleven minutes to "net" a steer. It didn't. Darned if that lasso didn't go around that steer's neck the first time out, and darned if Scott didn't hold on to that pole so tight the rope slid through without a problem. Of course, there was no way he could catch the end of it as it exited the pole, but that wasn't the point. She'd bet him he couldn't rope a steer. Well, he had. In less than a minute.

Just like he'd made you scream out his name in less than a minute.

She almost covered her ears with her hands. But she refused to let anyone see how losing her bet made her feel.

Disappointed. Frustrated. *Excited.*

Chase looked over at her, his face expressionless as he said, "Guess you're going on a date."

I guess I am, she thought as she watched Scott turn

Houdini toward the barn without a glance in her direction. *And I guess I'm not getting the ranch back.*

THERE WAS A BOX on her bed when Amanda got back to her room.

Sure, she didn't know until she opened the gray box that it was a dress, but she had a good idea because on the outside, in white fancy lettering, were the words *Saks Fifth Avenue*.

Saks, no less.

Sure enough, when she pulled back the tissue paper, a black silk dress and matching black shoes sat there like costly jewels, both of which looked fragile, but had probably set Scott back a small fortune. She checked the label—designer, of course. Oh, and it just happened to be her size.

Of course.

Oh, but it burned her up. Gone went her disappointment at not winning the ranch back. In its place was something awfully close to anger. Overconfident, egotistical male.

She scooped the box up, storming out of her room, down the hall and out the front door. Her boots must have smashed the gravel to smithereens.

These boots are made for stompin', and that's just what she'd do. Today these boots were going to stomp all over you.

Scott Beringer.

Mr. Scott Beringer…was gone.

She pulled up short when she hit the porch, the *whump-whump-whump* of helicopter blades filling her ears. Stephanie, Chase and her dad were all lined up along the rail of the arena, hands shielding their eyes as they stared at the departing helicopter.

"What the—"

She couldn't believe it. He was *leaving?*

"Oh, my gosh, Amanda," Stephanie called when she spied her standing there—likely with her mouth hanging open—the sound of Scott's toy fading into the distance. "Can you imagine having your own helicopter? I can't believe you're going on a date with him. What if the two of you get married?"

Married?

"I'm not going to marry him," Amanda all but shouted.

"Well, I don't know why you wouldn't, if he asks, that is."

How about I won't marry him because he doesn't have a clue about ranch life?

How about because he lives a life of helicopters and homes in Aspen and France and goodness knew what else?

How about because she'd tried once before to have a relationship with a man like Scott and it hadn't worked out.

"I'd rather marry a hippopotamus," she muttered. And she really meant it. She truly did.

IN THE END, SHE CHICKENED out on not wearing the dress. She had no idea where a man like Scott Beringer would take her, and showing up in a denim skirt and a white cotton shirt—which was about the dressiest thing she owned right now—to Viva La Fancy Restaurant where everyone would stare at her as if she was some hick from the sticks, which she was, she admitted proudly, wasn't her idea of fun. Still, in a fit of rebellion, she wore black cowboy boots with a swirled pattern of leaves sewn into the calf. It probably looked hokey, but she didn't care. Scott needed to remember she was no society girl.

You could take the girl out of the country…

And yet…and yet…as she stood there waiting for the helicopter to come pick her up, her skin tingled with a current of—oh, for pity's sake—excitement.

Oh, no, she warned herself. Oh, no, you're not going to get your head turned by a fancy dress and a helicopter ride, are you?

She wasn't, she told herself. She wasn't, she wasn't, she wasn't.

And then she heard that helicopter come in low and loud, and her stomach did that…that tingly thing that made her abdomen muscles constrict.

You *are* excited, she accused herself.

And she was, darn it, she was. In the distance the drone had become a steady hum, signaling a landing. What the heck was she supposed to do? Go outside? Meet him at the landing pad, er, pasture? What?

In the end, she waited. If he wanted a date, he'd have to treat it like one…helicopter and all.

When a knock sounded on the door, she called out, "Who is it?"

No answer.

Fine. She stomped down the hall, those darn butterflies returning, opened the door and said, "If you're selling cosmetics, I don't want any."

But then her eyes did a bottle-fly bulge because her first glimpse of Scott Beringer standing there with a dozen red roses in his left hand, a box of chocolates under his other arm, just about made her gasp out loud. Lord above, the man cleaned up good. Better than good. He looked—and she couldn't believe she was about to admit this—but he looked like that poster hanging outside the tuxedo store in town, right down to the sexy black tux with a stark white shirt whose buttons were cleverly concealed behind a strip of white fabric, with the exception of a single black one at the very, very top.

One she wanted to undo.

Slowly.

Lord, he'd even done a George Clooney slick-back to his hair.

What the heck had happened? Where was the geek? The glasses? The goofy clothes?

"No cosmetics," he said with a smile, white teeth flashing. "You don't need any." He gave her a once-over, Amanda's skin tingling wherever his eyes lingered. Nerves, she told herself. Just nerves.

"Nice boots," he commented. And he wasn't being sarcastic. He appeared to genuinely like her rebellious touch.

Get a hold of yourself, Amanda. A wolf is still a wolf even after he's had a bath.

So she straightened, called out, "Dad, I'm leaving," to wherever her dad was, then looked Scott squarely in the eye and said, "Well, let's get this over with."

Chapter Twelve

She felt like Cinderella.

It was the only way to describe how Amanda felt as she walked toward the helicopter. She was only missing the glass slipper. She had the carriage…well, helicopter. And she had the princely business tycoon on her arm. But she didn't expect a happily ever after, that was for sure.

Still, as she took her seat in a helicopter that had a passenger area about the width of her front porch, she couldn't help but peek outside the window to her left. And as she clicked the belt into place, she couldn't help but think how nice it'd be to have so much money. And as she tried to ignore Scott sitting next to her, his left arm sharing space with her right, she couldn't help but wonder if he took it all for granted.

Yeah, well, Amanda, wouldn't you?

And Amanda decided she wouldn't. Not ever.

"Ready?" the pilot asked as he glanced back at the two of them.

"As I'll ever be," Amanda answered.

"You strapped in, Mr. Beringer?"

Mr. Beringer? It sounded so formal.

"Go," he said.

Go…an order, not a request.

The pilot did something up front and a low hum filled the cabin. At first Amanda didn't notice anything different. Then a movement outside the helicopter caught her attention as, from her small window to her left, she could see the rotor begin to spin.

They were taking off. She was really going on a helicopter ride with Scott Beringer.

Slowly the helicopter began to sway. That was the only way to describe it. That or they were inside a giant Hula Hoop. The helicopter began to gyrate. First slowly, then faster and faster, the hum turning into a whine that climbed higher and higher until it passed out of her ear's range of hearing.

Hot damn.

She all but wiggled in her seat, Scott completely forgotten. Well, not really, because she'd noticed when he'd taken a seat next to her that he smelled good. Really, really good. Like expensive pine trees. If trees could be expensive.

"Here we go," the pilot said.

They lurched. The back end began to move around, then the helicopter lifted off so smoothly, Amanda hardly even noticed it. They began to climb. Higher and higher. She could see the ranch, the pens with the steers and bulls, the arena and…

Dad?

Yup, that was her father out in front of the horse barn waving up at her with his hat, his gray hair looking more white from up above.

Only when she leaned back did she realize she had a smile on her face. A huge smile. And who could blame her? Heck, she'd never been in a helicopter before. And she never would again.

"You like it?" Scott asked, his breath brushing her ear in a way that made her shiver.

"It's all right."

"Cold?"

"No."

"Positive?"

"I'm positive."

"Good, then look," he said, his arm coming out in front of her to point out the window.

"Oh, my gosh," she gasped, for now that they'd climbed a bit more, she could see a blazing orange sun dipping behind the mountains of the Bay Area. See clouds that gleamed off in the distance like a giant piece of gold, the sky above an egg-shell blue and then an orange and then a fiery red that seemed to paint the mountains and the Bay Area in pink.

"Beautiful," she murmured.

It was. They were coasting over rolling hills and it took her breath away, especially when they seemed to swoop upward, and then suddenly downward, her stomach lurching as she clutched at something to hold onto, found Scott's arm and quickly let it go.

"Was that a laugh?" Scott asked.

Had she giggled? "No."

"Yes, it was."

It was, she admitted. And she didn't care that he knew it.

"Do you see the bay?"

She followed his gaze, her smile no doubt one of wonder as she stared at the strip of water that glowed like liquid mercury. Had they already reached the Bay Area? Man, she was going to have to get herself one of these things.

"There's some fog hugging the city's north side, but other than that, it's clear as a bell," the pilot said. "Should look pretty when we get there."

The city. San Francisco. They were going to San Francisco. She should have figured. Why else would Scott have bought her a fancy designer gown and shoes? For a moment she wondered what the heck she was doing in a helicopter with one of America's wealthiest men.

You lost a bet, remember?

Oh, yeah.

And then the pilot turned the craft and Amanda got her first glimpse of the Bay Area from the air...well, other than when she rode in a jet. Wow. Oh, wow. If the sunset had looked pretty behind the Los Molina foothills, it looked even more stunning with San Francisco as a backdrop.

Fog hung over the back side of the city, but that didn't stop the sun from turning the tips of tall skyscrapers a gold and red that looked too vivid to be painted by nature's hand. And though from their height the sun still shone, beneath them it didn't, and so lights began to twinkle on, first from a steady stream of cars that crossed the Bay Bridge and then inside the office complexes that made up San Francisco's east side.

The helicopter rotated around, Amanda looking toward San Francisco and wondering which building they would land on, and how safe it would be, and if her cowboy boots looked stupid and a whole host of other things that had her edgier and edgier by the minute.

Only they didn't fly toward San Francisco.

She sat up a bit, wondering where the heck they were going: San Jose? Over the hill to Santa Cruz?

They headed back toward Los Molina.

"Scott," she drawled out in a pique-filled voice. "Where the heck are you taking me?"

"Burger Barn."

SCOTT ALMOST LAUGHED at the way she jerked in her seat to face him. The sun had just about set, but there was enough light left to illuminate that gorgeous skin of hers and her fiery red hair. "You're taking me to Burger Barn? *Burger Barn?*"

"You said that was your favorite restaurant."

"I was *joking.*"

"How was I supposed to know that?" he asked, trying not to laugh.

"But why the helicopter ride?"

"I was trying to impress you." And then he saw her lips twitch as if she were fighting back a smile, or maybe a laugh. "Did it work?" he asked.

"Yes," she surprised him by admitting.

Good. He'd worried that she might not appreciate his taking her to a burger joint for their big "date," but he'd reasoned it was her choice. But when he looked at her profile, at that smile she fought, making her lips twitch, he realized he might have actually scored points. Go figure. The first woman he'd ever dated who didn't want to eat at a four-star restaurant. And the funny thing was, he didn't, either.

When they hovered over the tiny barn-shaped building that housed Los Molina's Burger Barn, a lone street lamp lighting the barren parking lot, he felt more relaxed and at ease than he could ever recall feeling on a date. That shocked him. Sure, he knew he liked Amanda. Knew he wanted to make love to her, but he sensed in that calm a happiness and liking that went a whole lot deeper than mere sexual attraction.

"It looks kind of deserted for a Saturday night."

"That's because I arranged for the two of us to have the place to ourselves."

"You *what?*" she turned to him, her hair once again flicking him in the face.

And that hair smelled nice. Like the flower shop he'd bought her roses in, only better. "Paid to have the place to ourselves," he said again.

"How the heck much money did that cost you?"

"Who cares?"

Her brows went up, her amazing blue eyes widening along the way. "Unbelievable," he heard her murmur as she turned back.

Not really. As she'd pointed out to him not too long ago, anything could be had for a price. He'd simply asked the owner of Burger Barn how much money he made on a Saturday night, then doubled it. Simple.

They landed in a deserted gravel lot big enough to accommodate the big rigs that passed through Los Molina's main drag. Down the road a bit were other storefronts; Scott decided he could get used to the charm of Amanda's hometown. Cars slowed as they touched down, Scott saw faces plastered to windows, little-kid faces, and from nowhere came the memory of him being a little kid, of how he'd wished someone would come forward and claim him as his long-lost relative and take him out of foster care. Someone wealthy. Someone who would buy him a pony and a...

They touched down.

The thump brought him back to earth, and Scott had to blink a bit to dispel the thoughts.

"Do you want me to power down or come back and get you?" his pilot asked.

"Power down," Scott instructed.

"Might want to grab your hair," he said as he unbuckled his seat belt, then crouched down to open the door. When he turned back, he got the view of his life. She was crouched, too, only when she did it her dress gaped open around the neck, giving him a view almost down to her navel.

Hot damn. No bra.

"What?" she asked with wide eyes, a sure sign that his mouth must have dropped open. Then she glanced down, too, gasped, then clutched the dress to her chest.

"Pervert."

He laughed. "Just appreciating the view," he said, opening the door, which gave a pressurized *pop*. It was cold outside, and the air was whipped into a frenzy of dust and dried grass and litter.

"Close your eyes," he yelled over the sound, which was louder outside than it was in…an engineering feat that still amazed Scott. He turned to help her down, but she was already out, the wind plastering her dress against her body like static filled Plastic Wrap. Wow.

"Cold," she yelled as they darted beneath the blades.

Yeah, he could see that. "Should have brought a jacket," he called back.

"I didn't know I'd be running beneath the blades of a helicopter like some Bond girl."

"You look like a Bond girl."

They were out from under the blades now, the wind still kicking up the skirt of her dress. No, Scott admitted, she looked better than a Bond girl. She'd let her hair go, the rotors stirring the air with just enough force to make her hair ripple around her face, make her dress flatten against her sides, make her nipples stand erect.

Hot damn.

"This better be good," she said, rubbing her arms.

"Oh, it will be."

"I can't believe you closed the place down," she said as she fell into step beside him.

"That's not the only thing I did."

"What do you mean?"

He opened the door that was nestled into the long side of the building.

"What the heck is that?"

"Music," he said with a pleased smile. "Mood music, to be exact."

"Just what the heck kind of mood are you hoping to set?"

And then the strains of "I'm in the Mood for Love" must have hit her, because she rolled her eyes. Scott stepped back, letting her precede him inside, though he bounded ahead of her so he could see the look on her face when she saw what he'd done...or rather, what Burger Barn's staff had done.

"I don't believe it," she said. Scott had to jump around her at the last minute when she all but skidded to a stop. "What the heck *is* all this?"

"Do you like it?"

He watched as she looked to her left at a counter where, on a normal day, patrons would place their orders but which was now covered in white linen and roses. The members of the three-string band that had played at the barn dance were dressed in tuxes tonight as they plucked at their instruments. To their right, picnic tables covered in red-and-white checkered vinyl had been pulled off to the side. Except for one table, which stood exactly in the center of the room, with a white linen tablecloth, two china plates with gleaming silver alongside, and a candle that flickered and lit the table in a romantic glow now that someone had shut off the fluorescent tubes above.

"Well?" someone asked.

Amanda turned toward the counter. "Flora, what the heck are you doing here?"

"Working."

"Here?"

"Sure. You wouldn't believe the grandpas that come in here with their grandkids. Great hunting ground." She looked past Amanda and smiled at Scott. "Hi, handsome. Like what you've done to the place."

"You don't think it's too much?"

"Nah," Flora said.

Amanda snorted. Scott looked over at her. A snort? Had he actually heard her snort?

"C'mon," he said, the band switching to "I Left My Heart in San Francisco."

She took a seat, or a bench as the case may be—no chairs at Burger Barn—even as Scott scrambled to pull it out for her. She didn't seem to notice, just scooted herself under the table the way she'd done a hundred times before. Only tonight she grabbed a linen napkin that'd been shaped into a swan.

"Unbelievable," she muttered.

"I hear he's taking you to a hotel afterward."

"Hotel?" Amanda said, her blue eyes going wide as she looked between Flora and Scott.

"She's joking, Amanda," Scott said with a roll of his eyes in Flora's direction. But that didn't stop the wayward thought that he had that he'd like to go to a hotel with her. From the moment he'd first seen her in that dress, he'd felt the zing and pop that always accompanied looking at her. Something about the way she carried herself. About the way she'd donned her cowboy boots along with a two-thousand-dollar dress totally turned him on.

"Here's your menu," Flora said, placing a pink sheet of paper in front of them. "The crew in back thought you two might like something special to eat tonight."

Scott glanced down, brows raised. What was this?

Appetizer
Fresh Oysters
Heart of Romaine Salad

Dinner
The "Love at First Bite" Burger
French-Kissed Fries

Dessert
Seven Layers of Covers Cake
Whipped cream available for takeout

He let out a chuckle as he read the last, then looked up to gauge Amanda's reaction. She just shook her head, the candlelight catching on her hair so that the red strands almost seemed to glow and spark. The sun had long since sunk below the horizon, but the sky still threw a muted glow into the place.

"Why?" she asked, clasping her hand beneath her chin.

"Why what?"

"Why go to all this trouble?"

"Because I could."

"That's it? Because you could?"

He nodded.

She stared at him unblinkingly and Scott would have given half his fortune to know what the heck she was thinking. The candle continued to flicker, outside a car drove by, but inside a tension began to build that the both of them could sense.

Then Flora sidled up to their table and said, "What can I get you two to drink?"

"The champagne I brought, for starters."

It was as if he'd screamed, "My fly's undone."

Flora looked at Amanda. Amanda looked at Flora, then stiffened.

Scott said, "What? What'd I say?"

"I'm not getting in the middle of this," Flora said, turning around.

"What?" Scott asked again, meeting Amanda's suddenly pained blue eyes.

"I don't drink," Amanda said.

Chapter Thirteen

The music still played in the background, but Amanda felt as if everything had stopped. The time had come, she thought. Time to lay it on the line, because, darn it, he was breaking through her defenses. It didn't matter that she told herself earlier that she refused to be bowled over by what Scott's money could buy. That wasn't it at all. Rather it had to do with what Scott chose to do with that money.

Close down a restaurant.

For her.

She swallowed, and though she knew the words needed to be said, they still jammed in her throat like too many steers in a chute. "Two years ago I was involved in an accident, a bad one."

She saw Scott stiffen, saw the way his eyes darted over her face as if searching each feature on her face for confirmation of her words.

Amanda shook her head, looking away, her hand going to the stem of the water glass, twirling it between her fingers. "I wasn't driving that night, but I might as well have been."

"Amanda, you don't have to tell me—"

She looked up sharply. "Yes, I do, Scott. You need to hear this. Goodness knows someone else'll likely tell you if I don't. And frankly, I'd rather you heard it from me."

"I was dating someone back then, someone I'm sure you've never heard of but who was something of a celebrity around these parts. Jake Gramercy. Professional bull rider, bronc rider and anything else he could ride." Including other women, but she didn't say that aloud. "He and Chase were traveling partners, and if Chase wasn't winning, Jake was. They were good. Really good. And then the accident."

And though it'd been two years, though she'd gotten to the point that she didn't think about Rita twenty times a day like she used to, suddenly it all came back: the guilt, the shame, the horror of that long-ago night.

"We'd been drinking at the Spur. I must have had, I don't know, a few too many beers. I wasn't fit to drive and neither was Chase or Jake, but Rita, Rita was always the one who insisted on taking care of us all, only Chase wouldn't let her...not that night." She clenched her hands tighter and tighter in her lap, because maybe if she felt pain, the ache in her heart would somehow lessen. "I badgered her into letting Chase drive. Told her we were fine. That she had nothing to worry about."

"Amanda, if this is too—"

"No, Scott. You need to hear this." She blinked, surprised that there were tears in her eyes. "So we drove," she said. "We shouldn't have. I knew that. I was at that stage where you know you've had too much to drink, but you think you can control it." She shook her head—slowly—back and forth, back and forth.

"Rita kept trying to get Jake to pull over. I made her feel the worst, I think, telling her she worried too much and that we didn't need someone to mother us, and that was when she began to scream. At first I thought it was because she was mad at me. But see, she'd undone her seat belt to lean over the front seat. She was trying to shut the car off, I think. Only Jake swerved, and she must have looked up right when the other car was about to hit us because all I remember is her scream stopping abruptly. I remember Chase crying out. And the sound—" her fingernails were digging into her palms now "—I will never forget the sound. Like an explosion. Glass, metal, plastic, all of it flying around, and then silence." She looked up then. "That silence was so odd and for a moment I remember thinking that it must have been a dream—a bad dream—because it was quiet now. Then I saw the hole in the windshield."

"Jeez, Amanda." Scott reached across the table, his palm up as he silently asked to hold her hand. But she wouldn't give it to him. She deserved to relive the moment without support.

"They arrested Jake," she said in a voice gone raspy with tears. "Involuntary manslaughter. He's out now, back on the rodeo trail, but he's never been the same since. It really tore up Chase, losing Rita. He quit the rodeo circuit, quit life for a while. I did, too." She tried to tell him without words the importance of what she was going to say next, tried to stare at him unflinchingly as she said, "All those years I'd looked down on my father for his drinking problem, and in the end I turned out just like him. I let Rita down, let Chase down. And then I met Jake's other girlfriends."

He winced. She finally unclenched her hands, took a deep breath and clasped his own hands. They were cold, those hands that had been surprisingly gentle when they'd touched her earlier.

"It was during the sentencing that I learned that Jake had a string of 'friends' across the country who each claimed they were his true love. In the end I suppose it didn't really matter. The relationship was doomed to fail…like our relationship would be."

"Us?" Scott said. "Why?"

"Because I like you, Scott. Dang, but it surprises me how much I like you, given the low-down, dirty thing you did to acquire my father's land. But if you put that aside, in a lot of ways you're like Jake…always traveling, in the limelight, and I just won't put myself in that position again. Nobody with an ounce of sense would."

She stood. Scott stayed seated. "Chase told me today he'd take over your 'training' since it seems obvious you plan on keeping the ranch. All I ask is that you give my dad and me a week to get our stuff packed and a new place lined up.''

''No.''

''No?''

Scott shook his head. ''The deal was that you'd teach me to ranch, not Chase.''

''But Chase would be much better—''

''*No*,'' Scott said more firmly, though he had no idea why he pushed the matter. ''A deal's a deal, Amanda. I'm not letting you renege on this one.''

She lifted her chin, and he was relieved to see the tears had dried, tears, he admitted, that he hadn't liked seeing. ''And I'm not going to let you cut our date short, either.''

''What?''

''Sit down, Amanda. You need to eat.''

''Just who do you think you are? Can't you see I'm in no mood to consume food?''

''Fine, let's go.''

''Go where?''

''For a ride,'' Scott said.

''To where? I've already seen San Francisco.''

''And now I'm going to take you someplace else.''

''The only place you can take me is home.''

''Fine,'' he said again, getting up from the table.

''Where y'all going?'' Flora asked as they headed toward the door.

''She's not hungry,'' Scott said.

"Darn it, Amanda, you're not going to blow this, are you?"

"Flora, please," Amanda said, holding up a hand. "I don't need a lecture."

"No. What you *need* is to get lucky."

Which almost made Scott laugh, surprising because a minute ago he would have sworn that was impossible.

"Flora, if I were you, I'd worry more about your own sex life than my own."

Which made Flora throw a dish towel at her, making Amanda duck before slipping through the door.

The pilot was still in the helicopter, eating the last bite of a burger. "Damn, are we leaving already?"

"Yes," Scott muttered as he opened the door for Amanda. She didn't look happy. Well, after that maudlin tale, he wasn't surprised.

"Where to, boss?" Charlie asked.

Scott looked at Amanda, who was taking a seat.

"My place," he said.

"What?" Amanda said, turning.

"Charlie, start this bird," Scott said, blocking her.

"Not with me inside," Amanda said, trying to push past him. But there was only one door and Scott was in front of it, and he wasn't going to move. So he didn't.

SHE'D BEEN KIDNAPPED.

Why wasn't she surprised? Amanda thought as they crested the mountains that overlooked the Bay

Area. Again. Beneath them streetlights twinkled like tiny embers at the bottom of a fireplace.

Kidnapped.

Being taken to "his place," wherever that was. But she refused to ask. Instead she stared out the window, keeping her face averted from Scott.

Behind her Scott remained quiet, too, but she couldn't ignore his presence. She knew he was there. Over and over again she kept picturing the inside of the Burger Barn. What kind of idiot goes to so much trouble to impress a girl on a date?

Scott Beringer.

Yeah, but still…it had been a bit extreme.

You loved every bit of it.

She had. Darn it, she had. Who wouldn't have been flattered?

And tempted. Tempted to give in. To date him. To do…other things with him.

But she couldn't. as much as she liked him. As much as she laughed at his antics and was impressed by his willingness to work hard. So the question became, what was he going to do with her once he got her to his place?

She wiggled in her seat, blackness now beneath them, a wide lake of nothingness that signaled the Bay Area's west hills. She suspected Scott lived in the San Andreas Mountains. A few minutes later it was confirmed as they passed over another low mountain range and entered an area where an acre of bare land cost more than most ball players' salaries. The persistent *hmmm* of the helicopter's motor filled her ears as she leaned right and looked out. There were no streetlights except for those near the highway, just the occasional flicker of a house light visible between the tall pines and oak trees that covered the hills.

She was nervous. Truth was, she didn't exactly trust herself. There, she could admit that, too. Because that fact of the matter was, the whole time she sat next to Scott, smelled him, felt his presence, she was aware of him, too. Aware of him in ways that made her nipples press against the inside of her dress. That made her press her legs together as if she feared she'd suddenly jump him right there on the helicopter seat. Maybe she would.

No. You will not.

Then she gasped, because they'd climbed high enough to see over the mountain, the Pacific Ocean glowing like a sheet of aluminum, white-tipped waves visible beneath the glowing ball of a full moon. There was fog out there, she could see it to her left, only now it radiated a pure white that faded to silver and then dark gray at the bottom. They began to drop and Amanda caught her first glimpse of Scott's "home."

"Oh, my."

"Well?" Scott asked.

"PG&E must love you" was all she could think of to say in reference to the many lights that shone from its many windows. It was built into the mountain so perfectly, it was hard to tell just exactly how many floors it had, just that it was *big*. Really, really big.

And painted white, or maybe it was shell-colored. The moon distorted the color. As the helicopter touched down on a pad cut into the same mountaintop, a red air sock pointing south, she couldn't help but think that Scott was really, really rich. So she knew that, but this…*this* was evidence of wealth like none she'd ever seen before.

"Actually," Scott said, "I get a volume discount on kilowatts."

She looked back at him, and, damn it, it wasn't fair. Why'd he have to be so cute? So adorable as he gave her that boyish smile of his.

"You're kidding, right?"

"Yup," Scott said as he waited for his pilot to open the door. Who needed a limo when one could have a helicopter chauffeur?

Unbelievable, she thought yet again. As she thought it, she realized that there was a part of her, a pretty big part of her, that was impressed.

And seriously turned on.

She'd never been kidnapped before, and suddenly she was finding the prospect just a little bit titillating, especially when the door was opened with a pop. Scott turned back to her with a suave lift of his brows and said, "Am I going to have to drag you inside, or will you come willingly?"

Ready, willing and able.

"Willingly," she said over the sound of the rotors spinning.

He smiled, his lips tilting just before he hopped down and then helped her to her feet.

Spinning on her leather seat in a way that wouldn't shove the slinky material of her dress up too much, she told herself to ignore Scott's hands as she slid out, which she did, yelling "Where to?" above the hydraulic *whir* of the rotors powering down.

"This way," Scott answered, taking her arm…not asking for it, but taking it as if it was his right to do so. She told herself such an autocratic gesture should make her angry. What it did was make her panty hose melt. Well, it would have if she were wearing some.

She let him lead her away, telling herself not to gawk as she stared around her.

This was as far removed from the ranch house she grew up in as a Porsche was from a VW Bug…a very old VW Bug.

"So tell me," she couldn't stop herself from asking. "When you see starving children from Ethiopia, do you ever feel guilty?"

"Yeah, but I console myself by heading up a food drop once a year."

"You're kidding, right?"

"Actually, no, I'm not."

Which made her stare at his profile in amazement for a minute. Could someone actually *do* that?

If they had enough money they could. And Scott Beringer definitely had enough money. Nothing demonstrated that better than the house he led her toward, its stucco facade dwarfing her the closer they got. A path made up of granite stones led toward an entry obviously specifically designed for Scott's helicopter-commuting guests. Did he really have that many?

"Welcome home, sir," a bald-headed man said with a bow as the wood-and-glass door—with gold trim, no less—magically opened. The man's white jacket was obviously some sort of uniform.

"Let me guess. Jeeves, right?" Amanda asked as Scott stopped to let her precede him.

"Actually, it's Sal," Scott said.

"Oh," Amanda said. "Hi, Sal."

"Welcome, miss," he said with a polite smile. Not bald. There was a small horseshoe of hair that cupped his head, about the density of tennis-ball fuzz, less the neon-green color.

"Do you want a tour?" Scott asked.

"Won't that take a couple of days?"

"Actually, no, not if we skip the bedroom."

Something about the way he said *bedroom,* something about the way he looked at her lips for a second as if he'd dragged her off here to show her exactly that…the bedroom, that is, made Amanda lick her lips in sudden nervousness.

"Sure," she said, turning away from him and the sight he made in his tux. The black pants did marvelous things for his legs. Maybe that was it. Maybe she was attracted to him because she was used to jeans-clad legs.

She pulled her eyes away from Scott, finally noticing that they were standing in some kind of foyer as big as her horse barn back at home.

"Holy cow."

"You would know a holy one better than I."

She looked at Scott, blinked, assimilated what he'd said, determined he was joking, then looked around her again. The place was huge. Just huge. There was no ceiling above her, rather the tallest vaulted glass dome Amanda had ever seen in her life.

"You must be able to fit a huge Christmas tree in here."

"How'd you guess?"

Off to the left was an open area with walls of windows.

"Do you have those little moving sidewalks they use at the airports to keep guests from getting tired?"

"I thought about it, but we couldn't fit the machine that runs them into the basement."

She nodded as if that made perfect sense and as if he wasn't joking, which she knew he was. "What's down there?" she asked, pointing to the only normal-size hall visible.

"The maid's quarters."

"Oh," she said. "Because if you lived in a house this large, you'd have maids."

"Something like that."

She turned, her feet bogging down in the plush carpet as she crossed her arms in front of her. "And you want to be a cowboy," she said.

"I do."

"Why?" she asked, uncrossing her arms to motion around her. "Why do you want to traipse through acres of cow poop? To get up at the crack of dawn every morning to feed the cow-poop makers? Is it just a momentary phase?"

"I don't know," he said, taking a small step toward her. "All I know is I've always wanted to own a ranch."

"Wouldn't another ranch work?"

"It would if my selling the place back to you would make you happy."

Her breath caught. "You would do that?"

"I would," he said, closing the distance between them. And then he glanced down. Just a quick peek, but enough of one that she knew he'd seen her reaction to him.

"Darn it," she muttered under her breath.

"Darn what?"

"Why are you such a nice guy?" she said, wanting to cup his face in her hands.

"Is that a bad thing?" he said, coming nearer.

"No," she finally said out loud.

"I want to kiss you," he said while coming closer.

"That's not a good idea," she said, holding her ground, though her stomach had begun to whirl like a washing machine on the spin cycle.

When he pulled her to him, she didn't resist. And when he bent his head down, she didn't move. When he kissed her, well, that was the time to stop what was happening.

But when he kissed her, she forgot all about resisting. What she suddenly wanted to do was kiss him back.

Chapter Fourteen

Scott expected Amanda to pull away. He really did. But when instead she sighed against his lips, pressed her breasts against the front of his shirt and then kissed him back as fiercely as he'd ever imagined her kissing him, he knew the moment had come.

Then another realization hit him, one that blew his mind as he opened his mouth and sucked in her sweet essence.

He was nervous. *Nervous.* His hands shook as he lifted them and placed his fingers against the warm flesh of her neck, her pulse beating beneath his fingers with enough force and speed to show she was just as charged. His breaths came faster and faster as he greedily lapped at her mouth. His whole body flexed and then hardened as blood flowed so quickly to every part of his body, it felt like a rush of heat had hit him. He'd made love to women before, and yet, this felt like the first time.

Then she was pulling back, pulling away, and Scott

was filled with a disappointment that she'd changed her mind. Then she asked, "I suppose you've got a bedroom in this place?"

He took her hand. It was such a mundane thing to do, yet he couldn't help but feel a sense of pride that Amanda Johnson was finally going to be his. Not because he was wealthy, but because she desired him, in spite of the fears she had. He still just about ran with her to his bedroom for fear she'd change her mind, but his rush to get there made her laugh, and the sound of that laughter made a rush of something else fill him, something warm and tender and sweet.

"Slow down," she said.

"No," he answered, tugging her up some stairs until, thankfully, they reached his bedroom.

She stopped, her hand slipping from his grasp. He turned to see her staring around in awe.

"You have a whole floor for a bedroom," she stated, more than asked.

"Well, no," he said. "There's a bathroom and private spa and the tennis court over behind that wall."

"Tennis court?"

"Kidding, Amanda."

As he watched her stare around her, the fear returned that she might change her mind.

"What am I doing?" she muttered.

Then he watched her straighten. Watched her look him in the eye and say, "Maybe I just need to get you out of my system."

He wanted to laugh. "Maybe," he answered with a smile, but he knew it was more than that. He'd planned this whole date as a way of trying to "sweep her off her feet," as Roy Johnson had instructed. Only instead it was *him* getting swept.

He took her hand again and led her to his bed, his hands still shaking as he turned to face her and lifted a finger to one of the thin straps holding the dress he'd bought her. It slid down her smooth skin with ease. Scott repeated the movement to the other strap. He hadn't bought the dress thinking about what she'd wear underneath, but he sure hadn't expected her to be wearing nothing, and that gave vent to a burst of eroticism that made his head buzz. And when the dress fell, revealing Amanda in nothing but a thong— a cowgirl who wore a thong—and her boots, Scott almost froze. Sure, he knew she was beautiful, twenty times prettier than those so-called models he'd dated, but Amanda standing almost naked before him was a sight Scott could never have imagined…not with any accuracy.

She wasn't simply beautiful, she was…perfect.

"You're making me feel self-conscious."

He looked up, met her eyes, seeing her insecurities there. "You take my breath away."

She rolled her eyes. He cupped her face in his hands, lowering his face so they were almost nose to nose. "You do."

She didn't blink as she stared up at him, didn't

move as her pupils grew wide, and he realized in that moment that she thought she wasn't pretty.

"Undress me, Amanda."

She blinked then, her tongue licking her lips. Scott wanted to groan again, he wanted to take off his own clothes, he wanted to pick her up and deposit her on his bed.

He didn't move.

No, he savored the moment, savored each gentle brush of her fingers as she took off his jacket—the *swish* as it fell to the floor the only sound in the room, other than their rapid breaths. Then she began to undo the buttons of his shirt, first across his chest, then his cuffs. He enjoyed the way watching her made him feel, the way his manhood throbbed hot and heavy in anticipation of loving her, the way he could see her lashes flicker as her eyes darted over his body, the way her hands trembled as she moved her hands to his pants. The feel of her fingers there, tickling him, brushing him…

He released a breath, realized he'd closed his eyes, only to slowly open them again as she spread the fabric wide and let his pants drop.

He couldn't contain himself anymore. Bending down, he nipped at her neck, then sucked in the salty taste of her, his tongue fluttering against her flesh as he imagined doing the same thing to other parts of her body.

She threw her head back. Scott edged closer, their bodies touching for the first time flesh to flesh.

"Finally," he said, using an index finger to slide her underwear off her hips.

When she didn't protest, he almost groaned. And when she was naked before him, he found that spot again, that sweet spot where his manhood nestled and made him want to lift her up and impale her on his shaft. Now. This minute.

Instead he bent his knees, rubbing himself against the folds of her flesh, finding the spot he knew she wanted stroked as badly as he wanted to stroke her.

"Scott," she moaned.

He kissed her neck again, his hand finding her breasts. Too fast. He needed to slow down. This had to be good. He had to give her pleasure. Once. Twice. Maybe three or four times…then it would be his turn. Only then.

Gently, slowly, Scott backed her toward the bed, capturing her lips as he did so, his tongue slipping inside as control slipped further and further away when he kissed her with erotic thrusts of his tongue. Her knees buckled just before she sank atop a down-filled cover. Scott followed without releasing her lips, or her tongue, or without stopping his thrusts. His shaft found her folds again, those steamy, moist folds. At this rate he wouldn't last two minutes.

He pulled his lips away.

"No," she protested.

He'd closed his eyes again, he realized, had thrust his head back so that the hair at the back of his neck brushed the tops of his shoulder. He sucked in a breath, his nostrils flaring as he caught a whiff of her woman's essence. Only when he'd gotten control did he open his eyes. And the sight of Amanda Johnson as she lay beneath him was one he swore he would never, *ever* forget. Her hair lay beneath her, tighter against her scalp, loose around her shoulders. The sweeping angle of her cheekbones caught his eyes, as did the perfect shape of her lips and the amazing size of her eyes. Those eyes were black with desire.

Desire for *him.* Darn, how'd he get so lucky?

"Scott?"

She blinked, her breasts looking heavy and full while pressed beneath his weight. She was panting. He could feel her rib cage expand and contract beneath him.

"What's wrong?"

"Nothing's wrong." Except something was, something heavy and dark and almost sad. What? *What?*

"Scott," she said again, her shoulder flexing, her hand lifting to the side of his face. "Tell me what's wrong?"

He shook his head, smiling down at her to cover his confusion. "Nothing," he said, and then he shifted a bit, his mouth covering her left nipple.

She gasped.

The sound of that gasp, the way it hitched near the

end as he flicked his tongue against her hard little nub, that sound touched him in a way he'd never felt before, made him lean back on one elbow and watch as her head thrust back, as her body arched, as her hands dug into the covers.

"Tell me what you want?" he asked.

"That," she said as he played with her nipple.

"How about this," he asked, his hand moving down her stomach.

"Yes," she gasped as her muscles hopped.

"And this?" His fingers trailed lower.

"Scott," she gasped as his fingers skated around her woman's mound.

"And this?"

Amanda's hips came off the bed. "Yes," she gasped as he touched her like he had at the lake. Only this time there was no fabric between them. This time it was flesh to flesh. Hot, probing fingers finding her folds, separating them, dipping inside her.

She just about came apart. But Scott wouldn't let her climax. He seemed to know when to stop touching her, seemed to sense the exact moment she was about to fragment.

"Tell me when," he said.

"When," she moaned. "When, when, when."

He moved. Amanda almost cried out in protest. But then his tongue replaced his fingers and she climaxed with such force she came off the bed.

"Scott," she cried. "Oh, my gosh, Scott," she said

as her body peaked in a rush of pleasure. She didn't move, not wanting to lose that miraculous feeling, that throbbing release that made her feel like she floated in a never-never land of satiation.

Scott moved up her body, little kisses pecking her skin, leaving wet goose pimples behind. "That was once," he said.

Once?

His fingers found her again. She was tempted to tell him she didn't want fingers. That she wanted *him.* She almost ordered him to put on a condom and get the deed done, but amazingly, it began to build again: that feeling. She lifted her knees up, giving him total access as he whispered, "That's it, Mandy. Again."

Mandy? No one had ever called her Mandy before....

And then she couldn't think anymore because miraculously, she felt desire surge through her again, and then something more surged until she was calling out his name again.

"Amanda," he whispered, his breath washing over her. "I want you now. I thought I could wait, thought I could give you even more pleasure. But I can't—"

She felt him move, felt him poised and ready to take her.

She lifted her hips.

And then he was in her, filling her, and having him at last, feeling him inside of her after all the times she'd imagined it, after all the minutes she'd won-

dered about it, after all the days they'd been together...it almost sent her into climax again. But she
couldn't climax again, she was convinced of it, no
one could possibly climax...

Then Scott's hard body flexed above hers—and it
was hard, his chest sleek like a cat's, his shoulders
and neck bulging with cords of sinewy muscle. She
touched those shoulders, seeing the look on his face
as he took his pleasure, hearing the sound their bodies
made as they mated. Everything built and built and
built until she knew she'd climax again.

He thrust. She took those thrusts. He pressed into
her. She pressed back. He held himself against her.
She froze, too.

Then he emptied himself inside her. She knew it
because she could feel him flex, feel the heat of him
there...right *there*.

"Amanda," he moaned.

His pleasure triggered her own, only this was different than before, this was a fulfillment that went
beyond a climax. She took his seed, and as she did
so she felt more like a woman than ever before. That
feeling, that complete and utter surrender brought
tears to her eyes, eyes that she closed as she turned
her head away, Scott nuzzling the hollow in her neck.

What the heck is wrong with me?

There were tears running down her cheeks. Tears.

Because that had been incredible, she admitted. She
felt rubbery, like a balloon that'd been filled and filled

and filled only to pop, leaving behind a relaxed shell
that just sort of lay there.

You've lost it, Amanda.

She wiped at her eyes with the heel of her hand,
not wanting him to see what a baby she was by crying
because she'd just made love to him.

She'd been moved by the intensity of that love-
making.

And then he was shifting his weight. Oh, man, she
hoped she'd wiped the evidence away.

He drew back, and Amanda gave him an overbright
smile as their gazes made contact again.

"Are those tears?"

Dang. Dang. Dang. "No."

Amazingly, he started tearing up, too. Her heart
came to a screeching halt when she noticed it.

Oh. My. Gosh.

She lost her heart right then. Zip. Gone. Bye-bye.

"You're crying, too," she said, lifting a hand to
the side of his face, his razor stubble sanding her fingers.

"Who, me?" he asked as he dipped his head down
and took her lips in a kiss as sweet as he was.

Whoa, Amanda, the man stole your father's ranch.

Yeah, but she would bet she could convince him
to sell it back to her now.

*Is that why you did it? Is that why you slept
with him?*

No, she firmly told herself, opening her mouth to him yet again.

No. No. No.

He began to move inside her again. *Yes.*

Yes. Yes. Yes.

And then she forgot everything as they began to kiss and make love again.

Chapter Fifteen

Sore muscles.

That was what she felt the next day. As if she'd run up the center aisle of a football stadium twenty times.

Amanda rolled over, her head coming in contact with something that crinkled in her ear and sounded as if she'd rolled onto a bug, which made her jerk upright, her heart stopping for a moment, only to resume working again with slamming beats.

A note.

She'd rolled onto a note.

That made her eyes narrow a bit because there was only one guess as to whom it was from.

Mandy,
Have some work to do in my office. Join me downstairs when you feel like it.

There was no "love," no "miss you," no flirtatious remark about the remarkable night they'd spent. The tears. The sighs. The moans. Nothing.

What the heck did that mean? And she hated the insecure feeling that rose within her. Sure, she knew it was remnants of her relationship with Jake and what a hoax that had turned out to be, but still...

Shaking her head, she gathered the covers around her in case Scott should happen to walk in, which was really ridiculous in light of what they'd done together over and over and over again, but there you had it. Modesty prevailed as she headed toward what she hoped was the bathroom.

Amanda stopped dead in her tracks as she crossed before a wall of windows that revealed a butterfly-blue ocean off in the distance, white waves lining the vast expanse like line-ruled paper. To her left and right, pine trees centered her view, sticking upright like an expensive green frame.

''Amazing.''

With a shake of her head, she turned away, her toes wiggling at the decadent feel of the plush white carpet. White. It would last about a half a day on the ranch. And thinking about the ranch she'd grown up in, a house that'd fit in one tiny corner of this mansion, filled her with a sort of trepidation. Just where the heck did she think a relationship with Scott Beringer could end? And why the heck did she suddenly feel the urge to find that pilot of his and ask for a ride home?

Forty-five minutes later, showered and changed into a freshly laundered dress—did he have a dry cleaner's on site—Amanda opened the double door of his bedroom suite and paused. In front of her, curled like a giant ponytail, was a sweeping staircase that led downstairs. Windows surrounded her, the ones directly ahead showing her the Bay Area, a hazy brown sky hovering above a concrete sea. To her left and right were rolling hills filled with pine trees.

"Are you looking for Mister Scott?"

Amanda jumped, the cold zipper on her dress touching her skin uncomfortably.

At the bottom of the stairs, Sal stared up at her like a Christmas caroler come a-wassailing.

"Yes, I am."

"I'll take you to him, if you like."

"Oh, sure."

Her palms had grown damp by the time she came alongside Scott's butler-employee-whatever he was. "Has anyone told you you look like Mr. Clean? Only with a bit more hair? Well, not a lot more hair, but you know…a bit more."

She was doing it, she realized. She was talking a mile a minute, a habit of hers when she was uncomfortable or feeling out of place, which she definitely felt now.

"Actually, no," Sal said, cocking a look over his right shoulder. "And I'm rather grateful for that." He looked ahead again. "Please, follow me." In two steps he was ahead of her, Amanda thinking his shoulders were so wide, they should have a name written across the top of them, and a giant white number below that.

She crossed her arms in front of her, realized what she was doing and uncrossed them again. What the heck was with her? She'd spent the whole night with Scott. Why was she so nervous about facing him again?

Sal led her toward one end of the house, giant bouquets of flowers filling equally massive vases, the blooms filling the air with an almost sickly sweet scent. Lilies. Yuck.

''Here we are, miss.''

Miss? Pul-eease, she almost said, but then she was coming to a halt before double-width doors—because, hey, why use single-width doors when you had room for two?—and then Sal was stepping back, revealing what looked like the satellite communications center of a special ops team. TVs filled one whole wall to her right, office equipment such as computers, faxes and printers to her left. Worse, there were three men standing around a gray conference table. Men, not Scott. Scott was behind a desk as big as a flatbed truck, his back to her as he talked on the phone.

The door closed behind her with a snick. Amanda hadn't even realized she'd stepped into the room. One of the men looked up, the other two barely gave her a glance.

''Hi,'' Amanda said, feeling really, really...mad. Why the heck didn't Scott tell her he had people here? She could have at least found something more casual to wear. Maybe. As it was she had to stop herself from fidgeting in an outfit that was very obviously a holdover from the night before and that all but screamed "Last night's squeeze."

"You must be Mandy," said the one who'd looked up.

"I am."

"Scott said to go ahead and have a seat outside. He's talking to London right now. We have a new product that just came online and it's the end of the day there so he's getting feedback."

She nodded as if she'd known nine-o'-clock California time meant end-of-the-day London time.

"I'll just be outside, then." She thumbed over her shoulder as if there might be some kind of confusion as to which outside she meant. Stupid. The man smirked at her, and she could practically hear the words "country bumpkin" as he looked away.

Did he know who she was? Did the other two men who still hadn't looked up? Had she been dismissed as Scott Beringer's "country squeeze."

Amanda fumed. Not because of the way those two corporate suits had ignored her. No. She was mad because Scott had ignored her, too. The man hadn't even looked up, even though her eyes had gone to him once or twice. That burned the most.

So she waited, her reflection staring back at her as she stood ready to receive the big kahuna. Ridiculous, stupid, dumb thing to do…sleeping with him. What'd she been thinking?

You wanted to try to get him out of your system.

Yeah, well, that had worked well. *Not.*

"Hi, gorgeous."

She jumped, which made her even more angry because she couldn't believe how tense she was. She whirled on him, noticing how handsome he looked in a brown polo-type shirt that pulled taut against his shoulders and around the wide muscles of his arms and chest.

"Why the heck didn't you tell me you had other guests?"

"Guests?" he asked, his green eyes once again peering at her from behind black-framed glasses. "What guests— Oh, you must mean the guys."

The guys, she silently mimicked. As if they were a bunch of men who'd come over to watch a football game.

"They just got here," Scott said. "I had them come up when I realized I'd be in town for a while."

She crossed her arms in front of her, anyway.

"Hey," he said softly, "what's the matter?"

Everything. "Nothing. I just feel in the way." Out of place. Out of my depth.

"You're not in the way," Scott said, coming forward to touch her cheek. And that was all he did, touch her. Yet it was as if he'd kissed the back of her neck.

"I want to go home," she said firmly. She needed to regroup, needed to think about what had happened between them, or better yet, to get some clue from Scott as to where this would lead.

Alas, all he said was "Okay."

That was it. No "Don't go." No "You can't do that." No "Can we talk about this?" Nothing. And, Lord help her, it made tears fill her eyes. She looked away before he could see them.

"I'll have Charlie take you home."

And then what? Are you coming back to the ranch, too? What, Scott? What are you thinking?

But oddly enough, despite the incredible intimacy they'd shared, she didn't feel like she could ask him that question.

"Thanks," she said instead.

"You're welcome."

When she found the courage to look up again, he was glancing at his watch. His watch. Play it cool, Amanda. You don't want him to know that you're afraid it's already too late. You don't want him to know that while last night hadn't been all that special to him, it certainly had been for her.

"I'll see you back at the ranch," he said.

"When?" She couldn't help it…the question thrust itself from her mouth before she could reel it back in like a naughty marlin.

That was when she noticed that he looked uncomfortable. Or had the look always been there and she just hadn't noticed?

"Soon," he said evasively. "I've got some things to wrap up here."

"Oh, great, because Stephanie is serious about you riding in that rodeo, so if you're interested, you better come practice."

Oh, man, was that her sounding so grasping?

"Oh, yeah, right. Sure. Tell Stephanie she can count on me."

Tell Stephanie. Not her. "Well then, I'll see you later." She took a step toward him. He leaned down and pecked her on the cheek. That was it. No back bending, passionate avowal of love—not that she'd been expecting one. No lip-smacking, earth-shattering kiss. Nothing but a light peck on a cheek she was afraid would quickly be wet with tears.

And, darn it, but it shocked her how much that stung.

HE DIDN'T COME BACK to the ranch that day, or the next, or even that week. Oh, he called, but they were stilted, monosyllabic conversations that drove Amanda nuts and made her wonder how the heck she could have so misjudged a man. Granted, it wasn't as if he'd dumped her. He just made it abundantly clear that he didn't feel the same thigh-melting urge to be with her as she did him. And when she finally got up the nerve to ask him what was keeping him in town, he replied, "Business."

Business.

Jake had used the same excuse on her once or twice. But it wasn't until a few weeks after the accident that she realized his "business" was other women. Several of them, in fact. At the time she'd told herself it didn't matter. Only now did she realize that it *had* mattered. That deep inside, a part of her fear of getting involved with Scott was being on the receiving end of the "business" excuse again.

It didn't help matters that that stupid "Billionaire Bets for a Babe" article got picked up by the AP, appearing in newspapers across the country. It was exactly the sort of publicity she didn't want. Everyone in town, including the Biddy Brigade, shook their heads at her foolishness in making such a fuss about dating Scott Beringer.

So when she heard a helicopter's blades approach the ranch a week later she had to stop herself from running to the front door and racing to his makeshift landing pad. Instead, she finished packing the box she'd stuffed full of her father's belongings, then forced herself to turn and unfold another box, to tape the flaps closed with the familiar *zi-i-ip* of the packaging-tape dispenser. To straighten, to look around and observe what she was going to pack next.

She decided to leave, though she wasn't sure when exactly she'd decided to do so. It was most likely when she realized that asking to sell the place back to her would feel like selling her services for a favor. But it went further than that. Leaving had to do with pride. With the knowledge that sooner or later they'd have been forced to leave. Unless you had thousands of heads of cattle, ranching barely paid. Truth be told, the writing had been on the wall long before Scott had come along.

''What's this?'' Scott asked nearly ten excruciating minutes later.

She straightened, her ponytail landing over her left shoulder, every nerve flexing and then jabbing at her stomach muscles as if his voice were a pack of stick-pins.

She faced him, striving not to let the hurt and disappointment she felt show on her face as she replied. ''What does it look like I'm doing? Packing.'' Oh, man, had that been too snappish? Too curt? Could he see the gaping wound he'd caused?

He came into the house, a duffel bag of clothes slung over one shoulder, a black cowboy hat low over his brow. Back to Scott the rancher. How quaint.

''But I told your father he could stay.''

''My father doesn't accept charity, Scott. I'd have thought you'd have figured that out in the week you were gone.''

That was definitely snappish.

''Stop packing,'' he said, his Wranglers flexing as he bent to set his bag down.

''Not my decision to make.''

''Have *you* packed?''

''I sure have,'' she said, turning back to her task at hand.

''Amanda,'' he said. ''What the heck's the matter?''

That did it. She set the pewter figurine she'd been holding down.

"Nothing's the matter, Scott. Nothing at all. If you'd called, I would have explained—"

"I called."

"To say hi and not much more."

"Like I said, it's been a busy week."

"Yeah, I know."

"Are you mad that I didn't come back to the ranch with you?"

No she really wasn't. She'd known who he was before getting involved. Scott Beringer. Tycoon. Businessman. Sure, they'd had one heck of a night together, but she reminded herself that that had been an experiment, nothing more.

Yeah, *right.*

"Why would I be mad about that?" she said. "I told you on our 'date' that I didn't want a relationship with you. Spending the night together didn't change that."

But it did. *It did, it did, it did.* Couldn't he sense that? Didn't he know?

"I brought you something."

She stiffened, something about the way he said the words, something about how he held out a small box that could only contain jewelry—earrings, probably— sent a chill through Amanda.

"I don't want it."

"Open it before you make that decision."

"No."

So he opened it for her, a flash of morning sunlight from behind him catching on the diamond earrings and turning them into a quasar of color.

"Here," he said.

"I told you, I don't want it."

"Why not?"

Because she'd done some research on him while he'd been away. A great deal of research, thanks to the magazine articles Stephanie had clipped and then left for her to read. She'd read about the way Scott lavished gifts on his women. About the way he jetted them across the world at the drop of a hat. Just like he had her. Well, to the San Francisco Bay at least.

"If I accept those, Scott, I'll feel…cheap. As if you're paying me or something." She went back to packing, saying as she bent, "I refuse to feel cheap."

"You make it sound as if I'm paying you for sex."

"Aren't you?"

"No."

"Then there's nothing to talk about. I wanted it and you wanted it. Looks like we both got what we wanted."

"It was more than just mutual satisfaction."

Was it? Then why didn't you call me? Why didn't you tell me that before a week went by?

"You're right, it was great," she said. "But now it's over."

"How can it be over when it's barely even started?"

Because she cared for him. All right, so she could

admit that. But it was exactly because of that that she knew she had to break it off before things got out of hand. And though her ego felt marginally better that he wasn't giving her the cold shoulder…she knew that moment wasn't far down the road.

"Scott, I like you. You know that. But I'm not willing to commit to anything more than that."

"Who said we had to commit?"

Oh, direct hit. And the funny thing was, she didn't know until that moment that she'd been hoping he'd tell her she was wrong, that perhaps they could give a relationship a try. Only now she knew he didn't think of her in that way. He wanted to go to bed with her, and while the thought of sharing another incredible night with him made her body warm as if his fingers were skating along her flesh right now, she wasn't stupid.

"You're right. Who said we had to commit to anything? That's why I'm hoping we can be friends."

"Friends?" he said, running a hand through his hair. And dang it, she remembered what it felt like to touch that hair, too. Remembered what the skin on his cheek felt like against her own cheek. Remembered how hard and yet incredibly soft he could kiss her with those lips of his, lips that frowned now.

He looked away, shook his head. "I can't believe this."

"What can't you believe?"

"Nothing," he said with another shake.

He couldn't believe how it felt to be the one kept

at a distance? Was that what he was thinking? Oh, how she was tempted to ask, even as her mind and her heart screamed at her to tell him she was just joking. That she'd take whatever she could get, whatever time he could spare, however he wanted to give it.

Stupid.

So she went back to packing, saying as she bent over, "We're moving the steers off your land today." *His* land. It still hurt to say.

"A cattle drive?"

"If you want to call it that."

"Do you mind if I come along?"

Mind? Yes, she minded. She wrapped the statue with some newspaper, the sound crinkling in her ear like his letter had done when she'd rolled atop of it in his bed. "It's up to you. We'll be heading out this afternoon, maybe spending the night outdoors if we don't get the strays together."

He nodded, his hand with the hat in it hanging by his side.

"Then you might want to go into town and get yourself a sleeping bag and some other overnight gear. The keys to my truck are on the wall in the kitchen. Feel free to drive into Los Molina, unless you'd rather take your helicopter?"

"No, the truck's fine. If you don't mind."

"Not at all."

He stared at her for a few seconds longer. She could feel that gaze down to her boots.

"When do we leave?" he asked.

"As soon as you get back."

"Then I'll be right back."

And I'll be leaving right after the cattle drive. Come this time tomorrow, she'd be gone, living on a ranch in San Gabriel. And after that? Who knew? But she had a feeling her life would be far removed from helicopters and mountaintop mansions.

Chapter Sixteen

Scott almost cursed as he purposely stomped down the porch steps. Childish, but it felt good, his boots *clomp-clomp-clomping* on the wide plank boards like Wyatt Earp's on Tombstone's boardwalk.

Unbelievable. She'd broken it off with him. Granted, he knew he was partly to blame, unfortunately, Amanda had suffered the consequences of being involved with a business tycoon. But he'd planned to make it up to her. He always made it up to his girlfriends. Amanda was the first to refuse to let him.

He found her truck by the barn, the smell of her engulfing him in a wave of perfume that seemed uniquely Amanda, and that remind him all too quickly of how her scent had lingered on his sheets for days after she'd gone.

She'd dumped him.

He didn't like it, because even as he told himself he should likely be grateful she didn't want to try to lasso him like a lot of women did simply because he was rich, he didn't feel that way. What he felt was…miffed. Maybe it was the whole she-did-the-dumping thing that caused the chafing. Maybe it was because he hadn't been dumped since he'd made his first million. Whatever, as he gripped the steering wheel, he suddenly became…perturbed.

Scott Beringer liked a good challenge.

Two hours later, feeling woefully embarrassed to be driving a vehicle that he'd noticed had a license plate frame that read Wrangler Butts Drive Me Nuts, Scott returned to the farmhouse he now owned. In the yard a horse trailer sat by the arena, horses tied to the side of it, their reflection and that of the blue sky above shining back at him in the trailer's brushed aluminum surface. But it wasn't the horses that caught his attention, it was Chase saddling one of the animals up.

Next to him stood Amanda, her hair in a ponytail, wearing a pair of faded blue jeans that covered her long, long legs. Seeing her suddenly caused something to shift inside him, some emotion normally reserved for declaring war on a competitor. Maybe it was the way she stared at him so unemotionally, as if they'd never shared anything more than a handshake. Maybe it was seeing Chase in the yard. Maybe it was good old competitive spirit, but suddenly Scott decided he didn't want his relationship with Amanda to end.

"What took you so long?" she asked as he approached a few moments later.

"Traffic," he said by way of explanation.

She nodded—as if Los Molina had traffic jams, which it didn't—that ponytail of hers bobbing.

"Get your horse saddled up." Roy Johnson came up behind her, his thick denim jacket framing his belly bulge. He sidled past Amanda, an Amanda who had suddenly turned away, and moved toward the barn.

"What the hell'd you do to her?" Roy asked as he paused on his way by. "She's been driving me nuts. Nagging at me. Badgering me to take my medication. Hell, I'd hoped once the two of you got together, she'd leave me alone, but it's only gotten worse."

"She doesn't want to see me anymore."

Roy just shook his head. "Lord, I'm too old for this."

"I'm not giving up," Scott said firmly.

"I wouldn't have picked you for the job if I thought you would," Roy said. "By the way, she's leaving tomorrow after we get back."

Leaving?

"And stay out of my way," her father yelled, startling Scott until he remembered the act.

Leaving, he repeated to himself. She couldn't do that. Not yet. Not until… What? he asked himself. What did he expect her to do? Stay, after her father left? Ask him to sell the place back to her? Yes, he admitted, all of the above. But she hadn't asked for him to sell. That surprised him.

He got Rocket saddled up in record time, some of Scott's pique fading when he even managed to get the bit in the horse's mouth on the first try. Next he attached all the stuff he'd bought, a challenge in and of itself, one he managed to accomplish despite the bulky nature of the solar-powered cooker, the pots and pans and his solar-reflective sleeping bag. By the time he led Rocket out of the barn, he was feeling marginally better, something about being around horses had that effect on him, he'd noticed.

Feeling better, that is, until Amanda turned and asked, ''What the heck is that?''

Scott pulled Rocket up. ''What's what?''

Chase came up alongside of her then, his black hat pulled low over his brow.

''That,'' she said, pointing to the back of his saddle.

''That's my sleeping bag.''

''You're planning to sleep in a giant roll of tin foil?''

''It's a self-warming skin. Solar. It's made of the same stuff weather balloons are made of.''

Both she and Chase were staring at him as if he was planning on sleeping in a bed of snakes.

''And that,'' she said, pointing to a tall, thin bag tied vertically to the saddle the way Scott had seen cowboys tie their rifles.

"My solar cooker."

She and Chase's eyes widened. They looked at each other then laughed.

Scott just watched them, feeling as if he were ten years old again and the class bully had just given him a wedgy.

"I told you to buy a sleeping bag, not camping equipment."

"Yeah, but I'm a firm believer in creature comforts."

"I bet you are," Chase said.

"MEN," AMANDA SAID as she swung up on Fancy, and though she didn't kick her horse into a gallop, she did turn her toward the gate, opening it up without looking back at the three men who rode behind her.

She heard hoofbeats coming up alongside her, hoped it wasn't Scott...or Chase. And turned.

It was her father. "You and whirlybird man take the east pasture. Chase and I will take the west."

He was leaving her alone with Scott?

"But, Dad, I thought you could ride with Scott—"

"We can meet in the back-forty tomorrow morning."

"But I—"

"See you then." He jerked on the reins, his horse's head lifting as he turned away.

"But..." she called out after him.

Chase rode by, tipping his hat at her, feet forward

in the stirrups as he slouched back in the saddle and rode off.

"I don't believe it."

"Don't believe what?" Scott said, coming alongside her, too.

"Nothing," she said.

"What'd he say?"

"You and I are to ride the east pasture together."

"Really?" Scott asked.

"Really," Amanda said, kicking her horse into a canter, suddenly mad as a stepped-on hornet.

Men. If it wasn't Scott messing up her life, it was her father. She should just swear off them all.

To her surprise, Scott kept up with her. Granted, he'd never win an equitation class, but he managed to hang on pretty well.

Darn it. Why'd he have to do everything so well?

Like make love?

No. She wasn't about to go there.

"We have a lot of work ahead of us," she called out to him, her voice uneven with the horse's canter. And they did. Gathering cattle wasn't the romantic stroll through the park like the movies made it sound. It involved teamwork and coordination and nerves of steel when the time came to climb a hill that rose straight up before you. But it had to be done. The cattle were one of the few assets they had left. They needed the money from their sale to pay off other debts.

"How long's the ride?"

"'Bout an hour," she said, Fancy shaking her head as she asked to be let go. For a moment she almost did it, almost gave the mare her head. When she was little, it was her favorite way to forget her troubles: racing around the pasture at breakneck speed. But, despite Scott's improvement, that's exactly what would happen to him: he'd break his neck if she let their horses race each other.

So they rode, Scott keeping quiet as she opened a barbed-wire gate, then climbed back on. Yet as she worked, she had a feeling he was watching her, studying her, looking her over as if she were a complicated program he was trying to figure out.

That feeling only increased, so she finally pulled Fancy up, turned to him and said, "What?"

He lifted a brow, pulling up Rocket with an ease that took her by surprise.

"You've been staring at me the whole ride out here," she told him.

He smiled, a wide, warm smile. "That's because you look more beautiful today than I've ever seen you."

The comment melted her heart, until she reminded herself that that was likely his intent.

"Look, Scott—"

"No, don't say anything. I know you're about to remind me that it's over between us. A real shame, too, because I was kind of getting fond of the place."

She lifted a brow, and she must have clutched at the reins because Fancy tossed her head, the saddle squeaking as she did so. "Fond of the place?"

"Yeah. Fond of the ranch."

"What are you talking about?"

He shrugged. "Just that with your father leaving I don't have anybody to run the place. And since I don't have time to do it myself, as much as I enjoy my time here, I'm thinking I might turn it into offices for my executive staff."

"Offices?"

They'd climbed a bit as they'd ridden, the grass-covered valley beneath them a scenic view of gently rolling hills, and way off in the distance, the house she'd grown up in.

"I'm thinking I could put offices over there." He pointed to the left of the house. "Just a few offices, enough for my executive staff. Maybe one- or two-hundred-thousand square feet."

Two-hundred-thousand square feet?

"Housing's less expensive in this area," he added, "although now that I think about it, a nice perk would be to build them a house out here. Heck, maybe right even where we're standing."

She felt her mouth drop open, then snap close, then open again. It hung that way a full five seconds before she said, "You wouldn't dare."

"I wouldn't if you agreed to stay behind and manage the ranch. With help, of course."

And that's when she stiffened, when she realized he was trying to arm-wrestle her into staying.

"You're amazing, you know that?"

Now it was his turn to lift a brow.

"You're trying to blackmail me."

He shrugged. "You didn't think I got to where I am today being a nice guy, did you?"

Maybe she had. Maybe she hadn't. "It won't work, Scott."

"What won't?"

"Trying to force me into staying. See, I always suspected that one day this land would end up under concrete. This close to the Bay Area, a developer could make a fortune selling off bits and pieces of it, like my father should have done, if he'd had the money to subdivide it. But he didn't, and so I knew that one day it'd end up this way, though I always assumed dad would sell the land, not lose it to someone like you."

"Someone like me?"

She turned on him then. "Yeah, someone like you, Scott. Someone who uses the land as a barter for sex with a woman he desires."

"Wait a moment—"

"Wait? For what? For you to tell me that's not what you're doing?"

"I never mentioned anything about sex. I was just trying to hire the best man for the job, or woman as the case may be. I need you, Amanda. With your father's health failing, that makes you his best replacement. Without you, I won't keep the place.''

"It's blackmail."

"No, it's business."

"And that's what it always is with you, Scott. Don't you see, that's the whole point? Business is king for you. When you got caught up in it this past week, I was the first thing to go. *Pfft.* Shove Amanda aside." She waved her hand in the air, Fancy shifting beneath her. "Amanda won't mind, not when I can just make it up to her afterward by giving her some earrings or maybe a trip to someplace exotic."

He remained silent, and Amanda knew she'd scored.

"That's what you always do. I read about it, Scott. I read about the way you treat your women in every major magazine there is. You use them like they're part of an escort service. Call them when you're in town and you want a little nooky. But that's not going to happen with us."

"Research?"

"Stephanie gave me a bunch of articles she'd clipped. It's impossible to read about your life and not read about the women you've dated."

"And that's what scared you off?"

"No. What scared me off is that you've never kept a girlfriend longer than six months, at least not that I read about. You break up with them right around the time most men would settle into a relationship. Right around the time things might get serious.'' She looked him right in the eyes as she asked, ''Or is my information wrong, Scott? Because if it is, now's the time to tell me.''

Chapter Seventeen

Scott felt as if he was staring at a computer monitor that had just crashed. "How do I know, Amanda? I don't analyze every relationship I've had."

"No, you probably don't. You probably don't even realize what you're doing."

"Sally Bettincourt." He pronounced the name proudly. "I was dumped by Sally Bettincourt."

The look on her face changed to one of long-suffering impatience. "And how old were you when that happened?"

That she would pick up on that one little detail amazed him. "Old enough to get my heart broken."

"Mmm-hmm. But not your license, I'm betting."

One thing about Amanda, she wasn't dumb. Far from it. He had a feeling her IQ was right up there with his own. "I'm sure there were others."

"Tell me their names, the ones you got serious with *after* you made your first billion."

He furiously searched his data banks and came up

with…no one. Not a single name. That made him feel sort of clammy, even though he told himself surely there was someone…he just couldn't think of a name right now.

"I'm right, aren't I?" she asked.

"How do I know?" he replied. "I don't exactly keep a list."

"I bet you don't."

"And what's that supposed to mean?"

"Nothing, Scott. Nothing."

"Look, maybe you're right, maybe you're wrong. I don't know."

"No, but I know that if you and I get involved I'll have to play second fiddle to your business, or to your latest invention, or to your next public appearance. I've been on the receiving end of that kind of lifestyle, and I'm not going there again."

"That comes with the territory of dating me."

"No, it doesn't," she all but yelled. "Not if you care for me as much as I care for you."

"Care?"

"Cared," she corrected. "Because I'm not letting my emotions get any more entangled until you tell me I'll come first."

He stared at her. What could he say? For once in his life, he didn't have an answer.

"Well?" she asked, her eyes looking huge all of a sudden, and blue, and so imploring it made his throat tighten.

"I don't know."

"You don't know?" she said softly. "Well I do." She turned her horse and, before he could say another word, galloped off.

THEY FOUND THE MAIN HERD less than a half hour later, Amanda barely saying a word to him other than how to push cattle toward a small stock pond they were using as a gathering place. So Scott learned how to ride off the back end of a lead steer to get them to move, and as usual, he was impressed with Amanda's ability to do a job. She was quick, professional and a hard worker, traits he admired in an employee, but traits, he sheepishly admitted, he'd never noticed before in a woman he'd dated.

He pondered that and other things as they worked side by side throughout the rest of the afternoon, Amanda calling a halt only when the sun sank below the horizon.

"We'll finish gathering the strays tomorrow morning."

"What about the herd?" Scott asked, looking off at the bucolic view of a herd of cattle grazing near a pond, some in the water, some out, many chewing their cud.

"They won't go far."

He nodded, more sore and tired than he cared to admit. Amanda, looked her usual fit and energetic self as she did one of those sideways dismount moves he'd tried on that long-ago day when they'd had their first lesson.

Had it really been only a few weeks? It seemed as if he'd known Amanda a lifetime. And as he went about his task of unpacking his gadgets, unsaddling his horse, then rubbing him down, he found himself peeking glances at her from above the back of his horse.

She'd put her hair up behind her head in some kind of loopy knot that sent the ends of her hair skyward like a peacock's tail. On most women such a style would look messy, on Amanda it looked almost elegant. She bent over to set her own saddle and blanket down, Scott almost groaning as she did so. When she turned around, she froze, Scott trying to look away in time, but he knew he hadn't succeeded.

"What do I do with Rocket?"

"Tie him to that tree over there," she said, and he knew he was right, because he could tell just from the tone of her voice that she'd caught him staring at her rear.

"Won't he run away?"

"Your horse is trained to ground tie, Scott. If he gets loose, he won't run away."

"And what about you?" he asked, tipping his cowboy hat back as he did so. "Are you going to run away tomorrow?"

He met her gaze, seeing ire in those blue, blue eyes of hers, eyes that reflected the colors of the sky above them: the pinks, the buttercup-yellow and the deep purple of the atmosphere saying good-night to the sun. She looked amazing against that backdrop. Amazing and beautiful, and she didn't want a thing to do with him.

"Mr. Beringer—"

Uh-oh.

"What I do tomorrow or the next day or the week after that is none of your business."

Because he couldn't commit.

And that's when he saw it, that's when he noticed the way the rims of her eyes had reddened. The way moisture pooled in that little dip of her lower lashes. The way she blinked, then blinked some more, then finally turned away.

Everything inside Scott froze. He sensed there was a decision being made inside of him, a decision that scared the heck out of him, but one he couldn't ignore.

"Amanda," he said softly, going to her, gently turning her and, thank the stars above she didn't pull away from him. Her smell engulfed him, that floral scent that was uniquely hers and that filled him with a sense of comfort and peace. "It doesn't have to be this way. It really doesn't."

She looked up at him, and his Amanda, his beautiful, brave Amanda, had tears running down her cheeks. "Yes, Scott, it does—"

He cut her words off with a kiss, knew as he did

so that he was committing them to a course neither of them might like the consequences of in the morning. But he didn't care. Something about Amanda, something in the way she handled herself, in the way she proudly stood up for what she believed in, in the way she championed her father even though he'd disappointed her more than once in her life, something about all of that and more made him want her in a way that had more to do than with mere sexual desire.

"Mandy," he said softly, pulling back a bit, only to kiss the side of her mouth, and then her chin, and then the side of her neck. "Oh, Mandy. What am I going to do with you?"

She clung to him, even though when he straightened he could see there were more tears in her eyes. Her chin swang from side to side as she shook her head sadly. "How can I want to make love to you when I know full well that I shouldn't?"

"Because I feel the same way."

He did. He knew that his body might give her pleasure, but he was almost afraid to act on that desire. They might say goodbye tomorrow. He knew that, and yet he still kissed her again, still pulled the soft flesh of her lower lip with his own two lips, still pushed that lip down and then her upper one up, until they were kissing fully, their tongues coming together fiercely and in a way that led them to a place neither one of them wanted to come back from. Not for a long, long time, anyway.

Tugging her white cotton T-shirt out from her jeans, Scott placed his hand on her stomach, her muscles contracting in that familiar way. Scott's other hand slid gently up until he reached behind her and undid the clip that secured her hair, sending the whole mass of it falling down around her shoulders.

Beautiful. More beautiful than any ten-thousand-dollar-an-hour model. More stunning than those movie actresses he'd socialized with. More naturally gorgeous that any woman he'd ever seen.

She began to undress him—and Scott had a hard time concentrating on anything other than the way her hands felt against him. Only this time their coming together didn't have the sexual edge as the time before. This time they took their time, lingered over the undressing, stroked each other softly and tenderly. Scott was amazed at how her work-worn hands could feel like the gentle touch of a feather.

When they were both naked, standing there by the pond, the sun having sunk beneath the horizon leaving behind a muted light, they both stopped, both paused to look into each other's eyes, as if each gave the other a chance to pull back, to stop, but knowing that neither of them had the willpower to do so.

So when she led him to the bedroll she'd laid out already, Scott followed. And when they sank down together and made soft love, neither of them could ever remember feeling so perfectly attuned to another person, so physically excited by a person's touch, nor so completely frightened at what the future might bring.

WHAT HAD SHE DONE?

It was a thought that kept clouding Amanda's thoughts as she lay next to Scott.

"Comfortable?" he asked.

She nodded miserably.

Silence again, a silence that seemed to escalate Amanda's heartbeat the longer it went on.

What had she done?

Since the moment he'd come back she'd tried not to think about the way being near him made her feel—that exhilarating blend of desire and longing. She'd wanted him, never mind that she knew she shouldn't. She'd wanted him and when he'd kissed her she'd let him take her. Or she'd taken him. Whichever, it shouldn't have happened because now they were left with…what?

She closed her eyes, the flicking light of the fire still ticking her lids.

A mess. Now it was all a mess.

"Are you cold?" he asked.

"No."

"You sure? You're shivering."

"Rabbit running over my grave."

Anxiety, she admitted. Anxiety because she wanted to know if his making love to her meant he was willing to commit. If maybe, and, man, how she hoped the next was true, if maybe he'd decided to make their relationship a priority.

But he didn't say anything, just held her, his breath sighing into her ear. "You know, this is the first time I've ever slept out of doors."

She didn't say anything, just stared and stared into the fire, her thoughts going round and round and round as bright white spots danced before her eyes.

"I used to watch John Wayne movies or reruns of *Bonanza* and think, wow, wouldn't that be cool? To have a home that belonged to you and only you. To know that it was yours and your father's before you. To be able to look out and know that everything your eyes can see is yours and nobody else's but yours."

He moved, shifting her so that she was on her back and he was leaning above her. "When I was older I would dream of riding that land with a good-looking blonde—"

"Blonde?" she exclaimed, because she didn't want him to know how close she was to crying.

"Yeah," he said, his hand moving up to swipe at her nose. "I didn't understand the charm of a red-head back then."

Once again her heart melted because she could tell...she knew just by looking at him...that it was the things he wasn't telling her that caused him the most pain.

"Was it hard, living in foster care?"

He rolled off of her and Amanda missed being able

to look in his eyes, missed the comfort—however fleeting—of his warm body against her own.

"I suppose," he said on a long breath. "After my parents died I was too numb with grief to think about where I was living. Afterward, when I got bounced between families, I just figured that's the way it was. I think that's why I was drawn to watching westerns. The sense of family, the community, the lifestyle…I lived out my fantasies through movies."

She swallowed, staring at the profile of his handsome, masculine face. And though she knew to ask her next question would likely push him too far, though she doubted he'd answer it, she found herself asking, anyway, "Is that why you're afraid to commit?"

She waited for him to deny it, to tell her she was wrong, that he wasn't afraid to commit. Or more important, that he wasn't afraid to commit to *her*.

"Maybe."

It wasn't quite the answer she'd wanted to hear.

She knew she was falling in love with him. It wasn't because of his money or his house on the hill or any of the material things that stupid newspaper article had mentioned as a reason for why she should date him. No. It was because as she watched him talk about his childhood, as she'd observed him over the previous weeks, she'd seen in him a man who could be so much more than just Scott Beringer, billionaire. So much more. And he wasn't likely to ever feel the same way about her.

She sat up suddenly, clutching the sleeping bag to her breasts as she did so.

"What is it?" he asked.

She looked at him and took a deep breath, steeling herself for yet another question she knew she had to ask. "Tell me something, Scott. Does what we just did change anything between us? Anything at all?"

"What do you mean?"

She shivered with a sudden chill that she feared had nothing to do with the cold. "When we get back, are—" Dang, she couldn't say it. Despite how intimate they'd become, she was too afraid to ask it.

"Are we going to go our separate ways?" he finished for her. "Of course not. I figure we can split our time between your father's place and mine. Of course, that means you've got to unpack...why are you shaking your head?"

"Because that's not what I'm trying to ask." She ran a shaking hand through her hair. "What I'm trying to ask is if you think you could ever love me, Scott."

He just stared at her blankly. No, not blankly. He stared at her in surprise and then fear.

"Of course I care about you—"

"Forget it," she said, standing suddenly, clutching the cover they'd been using as she did so.

"Hey," Scott protested, having been left to lie there naked. "Where are you going?"

"To get dressed."

"Why? Because I can't say I love you?"

She turned and grabbed her clothes, slipping on her jeans and her T-shirt with more speed than she'd have thought possible with only a glittering fire to light the way.

"Amanda, don't do this. Don't make me say words I'm not sure I know how to say right now."

She whirled on him. He was standing, her sleeping bag wrapped around his lower half. A lock of his hair had fallen over his eyes, a day's growth of beard shaded his chin. He looked handsome and formidable and utterly masculine.

"But, I'm not asking for that," she said softly. "Or maybe I am. I don't know. All I know is I can't get involved with a man who doesn't seem to care about me as much as I care about him."

"Of course I care," he said, walking toward her.

"Do you, Scott?" she said, holding her ground. "Do you care enough about me to put me first?"

"Amanda, you're asking me to walk away from a company I've poured my heart and soul into. To step away from everything I know just to please you."

"No, Scott. What I'm asking is for you to put me first and your business second."

He ran a hand through his hair, shoving the unruly locks off his forehead. "Same thing."

"Yes, I suppose it is." She turned.

"Give me time, Amanda."

"Why? So you can change your mind and walk away from me six months from now?"

"You don't know that will happen."

"You're right, I don't. I just know odds are against me. And I can't live like that, not again."

"I'm not Jake."

"No, you're not. You're Scott Beringer, and in some ways that's far, far worse."

"Why?"

Because I could love you in a way I never, ever loved Jake.

"Because you're even more famous, even more wealthy, even more—" she searched for a word "—out of my league, and the fall would be long and hard."

She turned her back to him, turned because if she didn't he'd see that she was crying again, and if he touched her again, if he tried to console her like he had earlier, she didn't know if she'd have the strength to resist. She gulped air as she zipped up his stupid sleeping bag.

"Here," he said. "Use this."

As silly as it seemed, his offer only tripled the pain, because she'd heard him approach, heard him come to her, only she'd hoped he'd touch her—

"Thanks," she said, praying her hair shielded her

eyes as she took her wool blanket from his out-stretched hand.

He went to his spot and she went to hers. Alas, this wasn't one of Scott's silly westerns. There'd be no riding off in a trail of dust. The only dust around was the remnants of her heart.

Chapter Eighteen

They found the last of the strays in the morning, Amanda was in such a hurry to get back to the ranch that she didn't do her usual double-check to make sure they got them all in. Scott didn't seem to be in any mood to prolong their stay, either. He'd just packed up that silly solar thing of his, rolled up his bag, attached all of it to Rocket's saddle and mounted up.

When they met up with her father and Chase about an hour later, her dad gave Scott an odd look, one that made Scott shake his head as if warning her father not to say a derogatory word. In answer, Scott got a shake back from her dad, the two of them communicating in a way that made Amanda think there was more there than met the eye. But soon she was too busy trying to keep a couple of hundred head of steers going the right direction. To be perfectly honest, she welcomed the work. It helped her to forget for a bit that she was leaving the ranch she'd grown up on, a place that held both fond and bittersweet memories. To her left was the tree stump she used to jump her horse over when she was younger. Up ahead was the trail she used to follow to an old mining shaft that had long since been abandoned. To her right she'd chased a bobcat while atop Thumper right before her dad had sold him. So many memories. So many years.

And then there was Scott.

She'd silently cried herself to sleep last night, had torn herself apart and then glued herself back together again at least a hundred times. But in the end it all boiled down to one thing—well, three, really: trust, love and commitment. Scott didn't trust in love enough to commit to it. And who could blame him? She'd figured out in the wee hours of the morning that a man who'd been shifted around from home to home, who'd lost his parents and then lived in a string of foster families for all of his young life, really couldn't be blamed for shying away from love. He'd lost those he loved too many times for him to let the emotion get the better of him.

The stock trucks were already there when they arrived, their big aluminum bodies waiting to take the steers off to a sale, their plaintive calls to one another filling the air. As stupid as it seemed, Amanda found herself tearing up as she listened to those calls.

"You heading out?" her father asked as they pulled up by the big arena. "Because if you want to leave now, Chase and I can take it from here."

She watched as Chase dropped to the ground, hanging back a bit. Scott looked at her once, just once, as if giving her one last opportunity to change her mind, and when she didn't move, he turned Rocket away to ride him to the barn.

Don't go, a part of her said.

Silly fool, another accused.

"Yup," she said when she realized her father still waited for an answer.

"I wish you'd wait."

"Why?" she said with a shrug, meeting his watery-blue gaze. "I've packed everything there is to pack. The movers will be here next week. And what you don't want to take can be sold by that estate-sale company. By then you'll be settled into your new home."

"Retirement home," he clarified with a spit on the ground.

She smiled, Lord knows where it came from, but she did. "Retirement home," she said, though she couldn't believe her hyperactive father would hang his spurs at the Rosewood Community for Seniors...with Flora and the gang.

"You look ready to cry."

Gosh, she *was.* "What do you expect, Pop? Of course I'm sad. I'm leaving the only home I've ever known."

"You don't have to. Scott told me that he offered you a job running the place. It's not too late to take him up on the offer."

"No," she said instantly and firmly. "I'm not living on Scott Beringer's charity."

A car pulled up then and Amanda turned to see Flora pull to a stop in her new Camaro. Her heart stabbed her with a sharp beat. The Biddy Brigade. Darn it. She'd been hoping she could slip out of town without them knowing. Her father must have told them she was leaving.

"Amanda," her father said, catching her attention again. He took off his hat, a ring of sweat where the leather inside had rested against his skin glistening in the morning sun. "I know I've made some mistakes in the past. Hell, I still keep making mistakes. If I'd known how much this place really meant to you, I'd have never let the tax situation get so bad. I coulda sold off a couple acres here and a couple acres there, but I let it get out of hand, no thanks to the bottle you were always trying to take away from me. But I hope you understand, I never intentionally meant to hurt you. Never. You're my only daughter. Hell, my only child. You mean more to me than all the Sundays I've yet to live on this Earth."

There were tears in his eyes. Tears in her normally cranky, unemotional dad's eyes. "Oh, Pop. You know I love you, too."

They hugged until Flora said, "Get away from her, you old coot. We need to say goodbye, too."

"I smell," Amanda said as Flora enveloped her in a hug.

"We don't care," she said, drawing back to look

into her eyes, then looking over at the barn, her gaze obviously finding Scott, who'd cross-tied his horse in the aisle.

"You didn't jump him, did you?"

"Flora, if I did, it's none of your business."

"Oh, sure it is," she said, meeting her gaze with tears in her own. "What am I going to do without you, honey?" she asked. "This is worse than when you went off to college."

"I'll come back to visit," Amanda said, feeling as if she'd swallowed a whole bale of hay, and that she was allergic to that hay, too, because, darn it, her eyes watered up again.

"It's not the same," Flora said, and they both knew it wasn't.

"Are you going to hug her all day, or do we get a turn?" Martha said.

Amanda drew back and wiped at her eyes, which really did no good because they just filled up with tears again. Darn it, this was why she didn't want to see them, she thought as she hugged Martha. It felt as if she was losing her mother all over again. Three times over.

Edith hugged her next, the Biddies looking at her with a combination of pity, sympathy and love. Then Flora's gaze moved past her, settling on her father as if she were a Supreme Court judge and her father a convicted felon. "This wouldn't have happened, Roy, if you'd—"

"Flora," her father said, and that was a big part of

the conflict between the two. Flora always started a conversation and her father never let her finish it. "Don't start with me." Then her dad, her tough, hardened cowboy of a father, inhaled in a way that sounded suspiciously like a sob. When his eyes started to well, Amanda knew the unthinkable had happened. It was one thing to show emotion in front of her, quite another to show it to the Biddy Brigade. Her father hadn't even cried at her mother's funeral.

"I messed up," he said with a masculine swipe at his eyes, a clumsy, fat-fingered gesture all the more moving because they all knew it was rare. "And I expect you three won't let me forget it, either. Well, that's fine. I deserve your antipathy. Might even need your help with my drinking problem when I move into that mental ward you three call a retirement home, but not now. Right now I just want to hug my daughter one last time."

Amanda couldn't believe her ears. Neither could the Biddies, apparently. The three couldn't have looked more shocked if an alien spaceship floated above their heads. But that wasn't surprising given the fact that her father had just done something he'd never done before: admit he had a drinking problem.

"Come on, girls," Flora said. "Let's give the man some privacy."

Man, not loser, not drunk, not any of the other labels Flora usually applied to her father. Maybe her dad might actually make it this time.

But there were no words left to say, and when her

father enveloped her in another hug, they both knew it. When he pulled back, Amanda knew this was goodbye. She stiffened, smiled crookedly up at him and said, "Goodbye, Pop. I'll see you later."

He nodded. "Why don't you have Chase help you load your things?"

Chase did, though it didn't take them long to put six boxes, her childhood bed and dresser, and a few other miscellaneous items away. And then it was time for final hugs all around, although when it came to Chase, there was a look of amusement on his face, not sadness.

"What's that look for?" Amanda asked.

He gave her a grimace that she figured was supposed to be a smile. "Nothin'. I just know I'll be seeing you again pretty soon."

For a moment hope filled her that Chase might know something she didn't. Maybe Scott had said something to him...

But then she shook her head. Silly, stupid, unrealistic thought. "This from a man who's been thrown on his head one too many times."

"Yeah, but I still have all my faculties and something tells me you'll be back."

"You're right," Amanda said, choosing to misinterpret his comment because she didn't want to get in a debate about her relationship with Scott. "I'll be back to visit. Soon," she said, giving him a hug, and when she pulled back, Scott was there behind him.

Amanda's heart clenched to a miserable stop, then

leapt back to work as she waited for him to say something. Chase smiled again, stepping back, as did the Biddies and her dad, until all that was left was she and Scott standing by the side of her truck.

"So you're really leaving?"

She had no idea why those words filled her with disappointment. Actually, she did. She'd been hoping…

What, that he'd beg you to stay?

Yup. That's exactly what she'd hoped in one delirious, silly, ridiculous moment.

"I am," she said softly.

He came toward her, Amanda stiffening as she waited for him to touch her. But he didn't. He just stood there with his eyes peering intently down at her from beneath the brim of his black hat. And then he reached into his pocket and Amanda's breath caught again. Was it a ring…?

A business card. He pulled out a business card. And why the crashing disappointment *again* Amanda didn't know. Jeez, what a fool she was.

"Here's my card in case you lost the first one. Give me a call sometime," he said.

Amanda took great care not to crush the paper the way she had the last time she'd taken a card from him. Had that been only a few weeks ago? It seemed like a lifetime.

"Thanks," she said with a lift of her chin. "I will. And if I'm ever driving a helicopter over your house, I'll be sure to pop in."

He blinked, his eyes narrowing a bit. "That sounded sarcastic."

"Did it?" she asked innocently. "Gee, I'm sorry. I guess I just expected a little more from you."

"Amanda, we've been through this. You know I want to see you—"

"You're right," she interrupted him. "We have been through this before. And we both recognize that what we want from each other is impossible, though I suppose I have an easier time understanding your actions and motivation than you do mine."

"What do you mean by that?"

She sucked in a deep breath, which unfortunately only contained the smell of Scott, a warm, heady earthy smell that Amanda knew she'd never forget.

"Let me ask you something, Scott."

And she had to still the sudden thudding of her heart as she prepared to say her next words. "Have you ever *not* lost someone you've loved? Anyone?" she asked with a tip of her head. "Foster brother, sister…girlfriend?"

He stiffened, his pupils dilating, then shrinking to pinpoints as he blinked. "What kind of question is that?"

She moved away from him, though it felt as if there was an invisible rope that tugged at her as she did so. "Nothing," she said as she opened her truck's door. "And everything," she mumbled, feeling, darn it, tears fill her eyes again. So she climbed in, though her palms had turned sweaty and she fumbled with the seat belt.

She could do this. She really could.

Taking a deep breath, she turned. He stood by the doorjamb. "Goodbye, Scott. I hope you find a love that fills you with happiness, not fear."

"Amanda—"

But she leaned out, clutched the door and slammed it shut.

He tapped on the window. She started the truck, her ears still ringing from the obnoxious door banging. But she didn't care. In fact, she hardly noticed as she put the big diesel in gear, backed up and then waved goodbye to everyone, including Scott.

A Scott who didn't bother to wave back.

A Scott who didn't move.

A Scott who she would never, *ever* see again.

It wasn't until she reached the end of the drive that she realized she was sobbing.

Chapter Nineteen

As he sat down, his lawyers and CEO hashing out the terms of a deal that would make him an even richer man, his attention wandered again.

What was she doing right now? he wondered.

And had those really been tears he'd seen in her eyes as she drove off?

"Sco-ot," his CEO, Chuck Rogers, said.

Scott blinked, realized he'd been asked a question, then said, "What was that?"

Six faces—four male, two female—stared at him in astonishment. "You all right, buddy?" Chuck asked.

"Actually, I'm not," he said, meeting each of their eyes from across a glass-topped conference table that Amanda would likely think large and overly grandiose with its cherry-wood surface and matching chairs. He almost smiled.

"You know what, guys?" he said, looking at each of them one by one. "I don't think I care what you do."

Mary gasped. Chuck's mouth dropped open. Tim looked ready to choke on the swallow of vanilla-scented coffee he'd just taken a sip of.

"Where are you going?" Chuck asked as Scott rose from the table.

"To get some fresh air," Scott said, because they didn't need to know the truth. Heck, if he told them, they'd likely call him crazy. And you know what? Maybe he was. Just maybe he was.

TWO WEEKS.

It'd been two weeks and Amanda still couldn't get used to the concrete and asphalt that seemed to hedge in the very small ranch her friend owned and used as a boarding stable.

The L.A. sun beat down on her head, the habitual brown gunk that hung overhead casting everything in a murky glow. She hated that brown sky. At least in Los Molina the sky had always been blue, the grass green, the steers calling to one another in the distance.

Gone. All gone.

Her dad had moved out last weekend, the estate-sale company had removed the furniture. All that remained to be done was for Scott to level the place.

Scott.

Time was supposed to heal all wounds, Amanda told herself, but it sure didn't seem to be helping out this one. She thought about him at least a hundred times a day. Wondered what he was doing. If he thought about her at all. Probably not. He did, after all, have a business to run. He didn't need Amanda Johnson to keep him happy. And that hurt most of all, because as each day passed by, a part of Amanda always listening for that stupid helicopter of his, she realized it was over. Really and truly over. She just needed to get over him, too, she thought as she headed toward the main barn, a horse nickering when it saw her coming.

But a slamming door brought her up short, and when she saw who it was, she froze in her tracks.

Flora got out of her Camaro. And from the other side, Martha got out, saying, "…the most ridiculous excuse for a car I've ever ridden in. Don't they realize there's no leg room?"

"It's a sports car, Martha," Flora said. "It's not supposed to be comfortable. It's supposed to be fast."

"Out of my way," said Edith, emerging next. "I think I'm gonna toss my country-fried steak and eggs."

Amanda stared. Then she lifted a shaking hand to her mouth and began to cry.

"There she is," Flora said. "Look, she's crying again. Ah, honey, don't look like that."

"What are you doing here?" Amanda asked as she ran into Flora's arms. Flora, always Flora first, Martha second, Edith last.

"We're here to bring you home," Flora said.

Home?

"Back to Los Molina," Edith added—as if there was more than one home Amanda cared about.

"Though I almost feel like letting you go on without me. I don't think my stomach can take any more of Flora's driving."

"But—" And as much as Amanda wished for the windswept hills, rolling green pastures and blue, blue skies of home, she said, "There's no home for me to go back to. Besides, I can't leave. I manage this place."

"Pish-posh," Flora said. "Though I'm with Edith on the staying-behind thing. You, however, need to go home. Now."

"Is it my dad?" Amanda asked, sudden dread making her skin leach of color.

The three ladies looked at one another, seemed to have a private and silent conversation between them that ended when Edith said, "Guess we better show her."

"Show me what?"

Edith went back to the car, reached in, then grabbed something that looked like a folded newspaper. "Here," she said when she got back to her. "Think you need to see this."

Amanda glanced down at the paper, the headline jumping out at her.

Billionaire Announces He's Found Love.

SCOTT HAD NEVER BEEN MORE nervous in his life. From the other side of the chutes he could hear the crowd's roar as one of Chase's buddies caught a steer in record time.

''Do you think they'll get her here in time?'' he asked.

Chase looked over at him, and as had happened every time his former rival had glanced at him, that odd combination of amusement and disbelief filled his face as he very obviously tried not to laugh.

''You don't know the Biddy Brigade very well if you have to ask that.''

Scott nodded, the visor on his helmet almost clinking shut as he did so. He lifted an arm to stop it from falling, no easy feat since it was encased in a steel sleeve.

''No,'' Chase said. ''If I were you I'd worry more about what you're gonna do if those rain clouds over there come this way.'' He shook his head, that funny half smile on his face. ''Hate to see you rust up like the Tin Man.''

''She's here,'' Stephanie said, running up to them, nearly getting run down by a competitor coming out of the arena. ''Flora just called me from her cell phone to tell me they're in the parking lot.''

''This is it,'' Chase said, suddenly all business.

Scott felt as nervous as the day he'd chaired his first stockholder's meeting. To his right the Los Molina Fairground's grandstands were full, the whole town seeming to be present, more than one member of the press and assorted news stations present, too, all to catch live a moment Scott knew would make broadcasting history.

He hoped.

Though he was one of the richest men in the world,

though his face had been on the cover of more magazines than he could count, he suddenly felt like the biggest fool that ever walked the earth.

What if she said no?

You'd deserve it, a voice answered.

Scott knew things hadn't ended well with Amanda. She'd been right. He had been afraid to trust the feelings she raised in him. It blew his mind that she'd been able to figure out why. Then again, she was the only woman who'd ever truly loved him for him.

Oh, yeah, she loved him.

He was sure of it.

He loved *her.*

Scott gulped. This was it, then. The moment he'd been dreading and anticipating since he'd gone to Amanda's father and friends and asked for their help.

"Let me give you a hand," Chase said, which Scott didn't turn down. The two of them had become fast friends in the previous weeks, mostly because Scott realized the man wasn't the least bit interested in Amanda romantically. That had gone a long way toward paving the path of comradery.

"Here," Chase said, strapping on the leg armor after Scott had mounted his newest purchase—a white quarter horse gelding. When he was done, both he and Stephanie stepped back, the smiles on their faces all the answer Scott needed as to how he looked. Ridiculous. Outrageous. Romantic.

He hoped.

WHAT WAS SHE DOING HERE? Amanda thought as she walked toward the steep slope of the grandstand. Just because that headline had said Scott had found love didn't mean it was with her, did it? Maybe?

"Are you sure he's going to be here?" she asked.

"He's here, all right," Flora answered.

Something about the way her friend said that made Amanda sit up and take notice for the first time since she'd agreed to come home and find out if it was possible that the "unknown woman" in the article could possibly be her.

There were TV cameras all over the place. Of course, she'd been told by Edith that the press coverage for the rodeo had tripled thanks to Scott's presence, but that wasn't what tipped her off. No, it was the way those cameras pointed themselves at her, the way the crowd seemed to go silent when she climbed up the stairs and entered the stands from the right. The way hundreds of faces turned toward her, then just as abruptly looked away, as if it'd been choreographed or they were at a baseball game watching a foul ball.

What the heck?

In the arena, the action appeared to have come to a stop. Even the stock didn't seem to be loaded in the chutes, a rarity for a rodeo that usually kept the action rolling.

And then there was the band.

Amanda had never, ever, in the history of the Los Molina Rodeo—and she'd been to all of them—seen a band in attendance before.

What the heck—

Trumpets sounded.

Her heart leaped in her chest like a spastic puppy.

What the *heck*—

The announcer said over the PA, "Amanda Johnson, please report to the center of the arena. Amanda Johnson, to the center of the arena, please."

She knew.

Her heart fell out of her chest. Lord, Amanda thought she'd have to shove it back in. Tears filled her eyes because she knew. She just knew that the band, the TV crews and, yes, those ridiculous heralds who were walking into the arena on foot, long trumpets held to their lips, blazing red surcoats flashing, had something to do with her.

"What are you waiting for, hon?" Flora said from behind her. "Go on."

She turned, her three surrogate mothers, women who'd held her through the best and worst times of her life, came forward to give her an encouraging hug.

"Amanda Johnson, please report—"

"I'm coming, I'm coming," she called, wiping at her eyes, the imprint of her friend's arms still around her, an imprint she would carry with her for the rest of her life. But she'd only taken two steps when she was brought up short by the sight of a man in full armor entering the arena on a white horse.

Scott.

"I don't believe it," she heard Flora say.

"He looks pretty good," Martha observed.

And by now the crowd was into the swing of things. Every resident of Los Molina had begun to clap their hands. From the announcer's booth she heard a voice say, "Amanda, if you don't get to the center of that arena, I'll disown you."

Amanda looked up. Her father stood holding the microphone, his hand waving as he caught sight of her looking up at him.

"Unbelievable," she said.

"Go," people were calling.

Amanda went, slowly at first, someone coming forward to open the small gate near the center of the arena.

"Unbelievable," she said again, not even realizing she'd begun to cry again as Scott rode toward her, pulling his horse to a stop only when he was right in front of her. He lifted the face shield, and the sight of his green eyes, the sight of that small smile that tilted his lips and made his eyes crinkle at the corners had Amanda trying to swallow back a sob.

"Hi, Amanda."

That was all he said. Such silly words, ones that she would remember for the rest of her life…ones with which she would regale her children, and then her grandchildren. But for now she looked up at him and said, "Scott Beringer, you are one crazy man."

"Crazy for you, Amanda Johnson…crazy for you."

That was when Amanda realized that it wasn't some crazy dream. That he really was sitting atop a white horse, in what looked to be battle armor, while from the grandstands a band struck up a stirring rendition of "Cowboy, Take Me Away."

Unbelievable.

Scott must have been practicing because how he dismounted wearing all that metal armor, she had no idea. But somehow he did it, sinking down on one knee once both feet hit the ground.

One knee.

"Oh, Scott."

He reached beneath his breastplate with a hand that was covered in a silver riding glove. Her laughter turned into a sob again when she saw the small black box he withdrew.

He waved, and the crowd, the band and even the livestock went quiet as he said, "Amanda Johnson, I know we got off to a rocky start—"

Amanda covered her mouth with a hand.

"—I know you thought the two of us couldn't possibly work things out. I blew it. Afraid to commit, just like you said." He opened the box, where a diamond as big as her thumb winked up at her. "Afraid to commit until I met you."

He kneeled before her looking silly, ridiculous and more wonderful than she ever imagined. She had to all but curl her lips together to hold back her tears, as she heard him ask, "Will you marry me?"

"You know I should tell you no just to teach you a lesson."

"What lesson?"

"That you can't convince me to marry you with a suit of armor and a white horse."

The sudden desperation in his eyes, the look of fear she glimpsed there made her heart flip in her chest.

"What can I do to convince you?"

"Kiss me," she said softly. "Kiss me and never let me go, cowboy."

He stood with a squeak and a clatter that made Amanda laugh, and then he was kissing her and the crowd erupted into cheers as Scott used his hands to pull her up against him. And when he drew back a long while later, he said, "I take it that's a yes?"

"That depends," she said softly.

"On what?"

"On whether or not you agree to put me first. I can't live my life playing second string to a corporation."

"As for that—" he said, reaching beneath his breastplate again and revealing a manila envelope "—I have this to give to you."

She took the envelope, her hands shaking as she opened it, and when she did, she gasped yet again.

Deed of Trust.

Scott Beringer herein grants to Amanda Johnson that real property known as...

"Oh, Scott," she gasped, suddenly sobbing as he pulled her into his arms. "Does this mean—?"

He nodded. "I promoted my right hand man to president seeing as how I won't have time to run

Global Dynamics anymore, not if we're going to get your breeding farm off the ground.''

Her breeding farm? What? She drew back in shock.

"Your father told me," he said gently, obviously reading the question in her eyes. "And I think it's a great idea." Then he smiled crookedly. "Will you let me help you?"

She stared into his eyes, reading the seriousness there, knowing he was committing to her in a way he'd never committed to another person in his life. "Only if you'll marry me first."

And then they laughed, the crowd still cheering, her father grinning at them from up in the booth, Chase and Stephanie smiling from the other side of the chutes. But in the arena, Scott and Amanda hardly noticed, they were too busy sealing their bargain with another kiss.

Epilogue

Ten months later

"I can't do it," Scott cried as he raced out the door, hospital gown flaring at the back. "I just can't do it."

"Scott," Chase said, grabbing him by the gown's tie strings on the way by. "Get a hold of yourself. It's just a baby she's having."

"Yeah," Scott said as he came to an abrupt halt. "But have you seen a woman have a baby before?"

"Scott," Chase yelled, and when that didn't work, he prepared to do what needed to be done, even though Chase'd always been told by his nana Rose never to hit a man with glasses. The slap rang out in the visiting room area with a *snap* that caused conversations to abruptly stop.

It worked. The fear faded from Scott's eyes. Not all of it, but enough. At least he wasn't as white as the hospital's walls and linoleum floors anymore. "Thanks," Scott said, rubbing his right cheek.

"Don't thank me. Get back in there and watch your son being born." A smile flickered on the edges of Chase's lips as he tried not to laugh at the woebegone expression on the richest man in America's face.

"You're right," Scott said, straightening his glasses with his index finger. "I need to go back on...in," he quickly corrected.

Chase clutched Scott by the shoulders, turned him around, then gave him a shove toward the door. A second later, that door opened to emit Amanda's exhausted huffing, the doctor's calls to push and the Biddies murmurs of encouragement.

"You think he'll pass out?" Roy Johnson said from behind Chase as the gray door clicked closed with a sharp *snick* from its brushed aluminum handle and lock.

"I doubt the Biddies will let him."

"Yeah, you're probably right. Never met a bunch of bossier dames," Roy Johnson said. "They're constantly riding me about my health."

"It's worked. You look better than I've ever seen you."

"Yeah, well, I wanted to be around to watch my grandchildren grow. 'Sides, I figured I owed it to Amanda to get my act together after all that's happened."

Chase's nod of approval stilled as the sound of Roy Johnson's first grandchild rang out from the other side of the door. Actually, everything inside Chase quieted; he felt the oddest combination of awe and amazement as he listened to the exhausted cheers of those inside the room, felt, for just a moment, just the tiniest bit of envy.

"Guess I have a grandson?" Roy said, and damn it, the old man's eyes were misty.

"Guess you do," Chase answered, wiping at his own eyes. Furtively, of course.

The door opened, and Scott emerged, his eyes wide behind his thick black glasses that were fogged as he said, "It's a boy."

"Scott," Chase said on a laugh. "We knew it would be a boy."

"Yeah, but you never know—"

The door slammed closed. The two men started at it before erupting into chuckles.

But an hour later, Chase got to see for himself that it was, indeed, a boy.

"Thanks," Scott said softly as he gingerly handed the newborn to Chase. "For you-know-what earlier."

"No problem," Chase said, taking the boy, then studying what must be the world's tiniest hands—and even more amazingly—fingernails. "Wow."

"If there's ever anything I can do for you…" Scott let the words hang.

Chase didn't look up as he said, "Actually, there is." The two men's gazes met over the sweet-smelling form of a sleeping child with an amazing amount of red hair. "My nana Rose died a few months back."

Scott's look asked, "Yeah?"

"Well, it seems she left me quite a few shares in a company you might have heard of."

"What's that?"

"Global Dynamics."

Chase had the rum-eyed pleasure of watching Scott Beringer's eyes bulge. And he knew the exact moment when he put the two names together, too.

"Rose Cavanaugh was your nana Rose?"

"Guess you've heard of her?"

"How could I not have heard of one of our biggest shareholders? I'd heard she died, but—" And then Scott's eyes widened again. "Do you have any idea how much that stock is worth? It's split ten times since she first invested."

"Few million, the attorney told me."

"Unbelievable," Scott said, sitting back in his chair. "You're a rich man, Chase Cavanaugh."

"So I hear."

"Any idea what you're going to do with the money?"

"Not a clue."

"Spend it," a sleepy voice said from the bed. Both men turned to look at a doe-eyed Amanda, the baby stirring in his sleep as if he'd recognized his mama had spoken.

"Hey, gorgeous," Scott said tenderly.

Chase hung back, not wanting to interfere with the tender moment. As he watched Scott gently wipe away a lock of Amanda's long red hair, envy filled him again. Envy and happiness for his friends, and a whole host of other emotions he wasn't quite sure what to do with.

"Hey, Chase," Amanda said, meeting his gaze. "I see you've met our son."

"He's beautiful, Amanda," Chase said as he gently handed him to her.

"No, Chase, he's *handsome*." She looked up at Scott, smiling as she said, "Just like my husband, even though he's got some sort of red mark on his face. What the heck happened?"

Scott and Chase looked at each other, then they both burst out laughing, Amanda staring between them both like they'd gone crazy.

"See, your husband here—"

And when he finished there was laughter all around, a laughter that filled the room and the lives of all who witnessed it, and that never seemed to fade from the Beringer household, because it was a laughter born of happiness...and love.

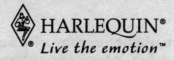

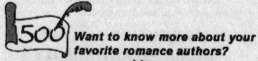

LEGACIES . LIES . LOVE .

July 19, 1983…

The Kinards, the Richardses and the Webbers—Seattle's Kennedys. Their "compound"—elegant Forrester Square… until the fateful night that tore these families apart.

Twenty years later…

Their children were reunited. Repressed memories and family secrets were about to be revealed. And one person was out to make sure they never remembered…

Visit us at www.eHarlequin.com
FSQ1OFFCOUPUS
© 2003 Harlequin Enterprises Ltd.

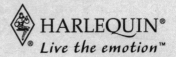

HARLEQUIN®
Live the emotion™

LEGACIES . LIES . LOVE .

July 19, 1983…

The Kinards, the Richardses and the Webbers—Seattle's
Kennedys. Their "compound"—elegant Forrester Square…
until the fateful night that tore these families apart.

Twenty years later…

Their children were reunited. Repressed memories and
family secrets were about to be revealed. And one person
was out to make sure they never remembered…

Save $1.00 off

your purchase of any
Harlequin® Forrester Square title
on-sale August 2003 through July 2004

RETAILER: Harlequin Enterprises Ltd. will pay the face value of this coupon plus
10.25¢ if submitted by customer for this product only. Any other use constitutes fraud.
Coupon is nonassignable. Void if taxed, prohibited or restricted by law. Void if copied.
Consumer must pay any government taxes. Valid in Canada only. Nielson Clearing
House customers—mail to: Harlequin Enterprises Ltd., 661 Millidge Avenue, P.O. Box
639, Saint John, N.B. E2L 4A5. Non NCH retailer—for reimbursement submit coupons
and proof of sales directly to: Harlequin Enterprises Ltd., Retail Sales Dept., 225
Duncan Mill Rd., Don Mills, Ontario M3B 3K9, Canada.

Coupon expires July 30, 2004.
Redeemable at participating retail outlets in Canada only.
Limit one coupon per purchase.

52605231

Visit us at www.eHarlequin.com
FSQ1OFFCOUPCAN
© 2003 Harlequin Enterprises Ltd.

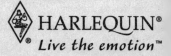

Your opinion is important to us! Please take a few moments to share your thoughts with us about your experiences with Harlequin and Silhouette books. Your comments will be very useful in ensuring that we deliver books you love to read.
Please take a few minutes to complete the questionnaire, then send it to us at the address below.

Send your completed questionnaires to:
Harlequin/Silhouette Reader Survey, P.O. Box 9046, Buffalo, NY 14269-9046

---

1. As you may know, there are many different lines under the Harlequin and Silhouette brands. Each of the lines is listed below. Please check the box that most represents your reading habit for each line.

Line	Currently read this line	Do not read this line	Not sure if I read this line
Harlequin American Romance	❏	❏	❏
Harlequin Duets	❏	❏	❏
Harlequin Romance	❏	❏	❏
Harlequin Historicals	❏	❏	❏
Harlequin Superromance	❏	❏	❏
Harlequin Intrigue	❏	❏	❏
Harlequin Presents	❏	❏	❏
Harlequin Temptation	❏	❏	❏
Harlequin Blaze	❏	❏	❏
Silhouette Special Edition	❏	❏	❏
Silhouette Romance	❏	❏	❏
Silhouette Intimate Moments	❏	❏	❏
Silhouette Desire	❏	❏	❏

2. Which of the following best describes why you bought *this book?* One answer only, please.

the picture on the cover	❏	the title	❏
the author	❏	the line is one I read often	❏
part of a miniseries	❏	saw an ad in another book	❏
saw an ad in a magazine/newsletter	❏	a friend told me about it	❏
I borrowed/was given this book	❏	other: _____	❏

3. Where did you buy *this book?* One answer only, please.

at Barnes & Noble	❏	at a grocery store	❏
at Waldenbooks	❏	at a drugstore	❏
at Borders	❏	on eHarlequin.com Web site	❏
at another bookstore	❏	from another Web site	❏
at Wal-Mart	❏	Harlequin/Silhouette Reader	❏
at Target	❏	Service/through the mail	
at Kmart	❏	used books from anywhere	❏
at another department store or mass merchandiser	❏	I borrowed/was given this book	❏

4. On average, how many Harlequin and Silhouette books do you buy at one time?

I buy _____ books at one time	❏
I rarely buy a book	❏

MRQ403HAR-1A

5. How many times per month do you shop for any *Harlequin and/or Silhouette* books?
One answer only, please.

1 or more times a week	❑	a few times per year	❑
1 to 3 times per month	❑	less often than once a year	❑
1 to 2 times every 3 months	❑	never	❑

6. When you think of your ideal heroine, which *one* statement describes her the best?
One answer only, please.

She's a woman who is strong-willed	❑	She's a desirable woman	❑
She's a woman who is needed by others	❑	She's a powerful woman	❑
She's a woman who is taken care of	❑	She's a passionate woman	❑
She's an adventurous woman	❑	She's a sensitive woman	❑

7. The following statements describe types or genres of books that you may be
interested in reading. Pick *up to 2 types* of books that you are most interested in.

I like to read about truly romantic relationships	❑
I like to read stories that are sexy romances	❑
I like to read romantic comedies	❑
I like to read a romantic mystery/suspense	❑
I like to read about romantic adventures	❑
I like to read romance stories that involve family	❑
I like to read about a romance in times or places that I have never seen	❑
Other: _____	❑

*The following questions help us to group your answers with those readers who are
similar to you. Your answers will remain confidential.*

8. Please record your year of birth below.
19 _____

9. What is your marital status?

single ❑   married ❑   common-law ❑   widowed ❑
divorced/separated ❑

10. Do you have children 18 years of age or younger currently living at home?
yes ❑   no ❑

11. Which of the following best describes your employment status?

employed full-time or part-time ❑   homemaker ❑   student ❑
retired ❑   unemployed ❑

12. Do you have access to the Internet from either home or work?
yes ❑   no ❑

13. Have you ever visited eHarlequin.com?
yes ❑   no ❑

14. What state do you live in?
_____

15. Are you a member of Harlequin/Silhouette Reader Service?
yes ❑   Account # _____   no ❑   MRQ403HAR-1

If you enjoyed what you just read,
then we've got an offer you can't resist!

Take 2 bestselling
love stories FREE!
Plus get a FREE surprise gift!

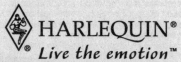